Pick Your Pleasure 2

Jayne Rylon

Pick Your Pleasure 2
Jayne Rylon

Published by Jayne Rylon

Copyright 2013 Jayne Rylon
Edited by Chloe Vale
ISBN: 978-0-9888124-3-7

Dedication

This book is for Chloe Vale. I couldn't have done it without you. The first time, or the second. I'm so glad we've become friends over the past year. I hope it's the beginning of a long partnership!

Also for Fedora Chen, proofreader extraordinaire! Thank you for keeping my mistakes from the final copy.

Table of Contents

Who is Henry? (1A)

Brooklyn should've kept walking.

Eavesdropping on Underground's owner and his right-hand man couldn't be good for long-term job security. Everyone knew Henry Emerson valued his privacy. Hell, she'd worked at his elite sex club for two years and had discovered next to nothing about the man. How could she when she'd said fewer than a dozen words to him personally?

Their lack of verbal communication didn't keep the hairs on her nape from lifting sometimes, right before she caught him surveying her from across the room.

Intently.

Despite how madly Brooklyn loved her career as a coach in the more advanced aspects of BDSM, and as a general guest host—which meant she got paid to party, or not, however she liked—her fascination with the man at Underground's helm grew by the hour. Maybe because of the animal grace he possessed as he stalked the floor of the club. His killer good looks hadn't hurt either. Dark hair cropped close was perpetually combed almost too neat with a hint of muss on top to save him from earning a reputation as totally anal. Rich walnut eyes she felt compelled to gaze into at every opportunity were impossible to ignore. And that body...

It was a body that put all others to shame when he strutted bare-chested through the sweaty throngs of a weekend crowd.

Vivid memories assaulted Brooklyn. She'd spotted Henry just last night, something about him even more fierce than usual. He'd flashed her his bared teeth, though the rusty gesture had probably been intended as a smile. Brooklyn had glanced away from the intensity of his stare, her attention catching on the ebony leather cuff he wore around his wrist. No one, not even her newbie guest, would have been foolish enough to mistake the adornment for a sign of submission.

Although Brooklyn typically liked to hold the reins in a relationship, she knew she'd let him drive her wherever he wanted to go. If only he'd approached her instead of maintaining that infuriating distance.

Unfortunately, he had strict do-not-cross lines drawn in bold slashes between him and the club's staff. At least when it came to playing. Though he sometimes treated a special guest to personal attention, even those occasions had been sparse—though spectacular—since she'd joined Underground's ranks.

Something was up with Henry.

It was in her nature to be the curious sort, especially when it came to human emotions and complex individuals with conflicted needs. He ticked all of her boxes.

So when she wandered past a seating area in the club's extensive gardens and heard two men who could only be her boss, Oscar, and her boss's boss, Henry, she slowed her steps to catch a wisp of their conversation.

Was it so wrong to ferret out even a sliver of intel about the guy who'd infatuated her from the start? She held nothing in reserve when she performed at the club. Henry—and Oscar, too, for that matter—had witnessed every bit of her passion.

All of her soul.

Usually, the brisk evening air helped her prepare for her clients. Calming her own psyche and focusing on external stimuli ensured she granted her partner's wishes, overt or subconscious, whatever they might be. Now, the close proximity to the object of her own fantasies caused her logical brain to go haywire.

Zen scattered.

Desire replaced it.

Instant arousal burned through her veins when she neared the subject of her fascination.

Muting the click of her boot heels by shifting her weight to her toes, Brooklyn kidded herself. She rationalized her stalking by convincing herself she was unwilling to interrupt the friends-slash-partners who seemed to be having a candid personal discussion.

Her gut told her Henry didn't open up often.

Through the manicured bushes, she took one peek at the strong profile she so admired.

A glimpse of the man who starred in her dreams? Check. A long enough look to satisfy any part of her? Hell, no.

Even so, she slipped behind a fanciful spiraled topiary, making do with the growl of his deep, smoky voice—a delight for her ears if not her eyes.

"I guess you heard I'm in the doghouse." Henry chuckled, making Brooklyn press her thighs together a little tighter.

"Exactly how pissed was Linley when you told her that you own Underground? Or was it your family fortune she flipped out over? Maybe the fact that you own the entire building her office is in? No, no, it had to freak her out that you weren't applying for the role of head of security the day she ran into you in her waiting room, but doing a real estate check of your own... I bet that was what put her over the edge." Oscar, the club's manager, gloated with his assessment. It probably wasn't every day someone put Henry in his place, and the manager was far too good at excavating information.

Oscar could read people like open books. It was one reason he insisted on greeting each guest personally. Every night. Preemptively discerning their mood and probable requests was both a skill and a delight for the enigmatic man. Plenty of women and guys alike had asked for him to be their Underground partner. Only, like his boss—more extreme even—he never indulged. At least not that Brooklyn had ever heard of, and she'd had her ear to the ground.

Too similar, these two amazing men. And still so very different.

Oscar, sleek and refined. Henry, suave though a little rough around the edges. Strong and imposing. A lion wrapped in fine trappings like his five thousand dollar suit, which didn't fool her for a second. It'd take more than fine fabric to obscure his primal energy.

Displaying some of his gruffness, the sound of curses mixed with Henry cracking his knuckles. "Linley threatened to eliminate me from her protection detail once she realized I'd never spent a dime of her paychecks and had been reinvesting my salary and bonuses in her company's physical and information security."

"So then she probably took it twice as hard when she found out…"

"I didn't share the granddaddy lie yet." Henry sighed. "One thing at a time. I wanted to give her a chance to adjust to the rest first. You know how much she means to me. As a friend, as *family*, not only as my boss lady. Though I'd like her to keep me around too. What the hell will I do if she kicks me to the curb? I couldn't chance it."

"As if you need to work." Oscar probably shook his head. "You've been watching her ass for years because you want to, not because you have to."

"I watch her back, not her ass, Ozzie," Henry reminded his second in command. He could never run the place without Oscar's help. Or maybe he could if his attention stopped being divided between Underground and Lane Technology. "Not that I'm looking. Ever. Shit. But I'm sure her guy would object to that in any case these days. Probably kick a man's teeth in for ogling her."

"Damn straight." Oscar grunted. Brooklyn could imagine his accompanying smirk. "I've never seen a man as possessive as he is over Linley. You may be out of a job soon, Hen. He'll never let anyone hurt her. It's not a problem anymore."

"As long as the girl's safe, I'm happy." Henry shrugged. "Mostly. I never had a purpose before her. Not one that mattered."

"So you'll have to find something else to keep you occupied. Though, seriously, I believe what you do here—the opportunities you give guests to explore safely, *anonymously*, and meet the partner of their dreams—that's valuable." Oscar got a little quieter. "You of all people should understand that."

"Exactly. My whole life, once friends knew who I really was—what I had—everything changed. It was wrong to keep Linley in the dark so long. But once I realized how well we worked together, I couldn't risk telling her and having everything go to shit. Like it did with Amanda...and Elizabeth...and Emilia..."

His string of women grew muffled, as if he dropped his head in his hands.

Brooklyn wanted to kick those bitches' asses for hurting Henry. How could they have been dumb enough to let something as meaningless as wealth ruin a relationship with a world-class man?

Maybe they'd given her a chance. From her own experience, she knew nothing mattered as much as love. Money couldn't buy faithfulness or the soul-deep yearning she witnessed whenever she glimpsed Linley and her lover in one of Underground's lounges. Now *that* was something to fight for. It reminded Brooklyn of how her parents had gazed at each other...before the accident.

"I understand why you took the approach you did with Linley. But if we're talking about other women, perhaps your strategy is wrong. Why not start at the club, where everyone's on the same footing and knows the score?" Oscar attempted to plant ideas in Henry's mind. "I know you're worried women like you for the wrong reasons, but I think between you and me, our bullshit meters are pretty well honed. Don't you?"

Henry sighed. "Yeah, probably. You could be right. Or I'm setting my expectations too damn high. There aren't many women who could put up with my diverse tastes, never mind *enjoy* everything I do. To find one who doesn't give a shit about how many digits are in my bank balance on top of that… It's a lot to aim for."

"Don't lose hope." Ozzie's reply came muffled, as if he'd angled more toward his friend.

The thought of Henry, vulnerable and needy, only turned Brooklyn on more. Dangerous with a soft spot? Yes, please. Sign her up right now.

"I could say the same to you, friend." Henry returned the club manager's sentiment. Brooklyn knew Oscar never let Henry down, always keeping things precisely in order. Yet, lately, they'd both been brooding. Maybe stuck in their ruts where before they'd appeared to thrive in their roles. If they were her guests, Brooklyn would recommend shaking things up and trying something out of their comfort zones.

Like fooling around with the help.

"It's impossible to find what you're looking for when you can't make up your mind about what it is you want." The greeter groaned. "At least you know you're searching for a woman. That narrows it down some."

"Nothing says you can't find a guy *and* a girl to keep you busy, Ozzie." A clap rang out in the still dusk as Henry probably connected his hand on his friend's shoulder. She could picture the gesture she'd seen him make several times in the past. "Why choose? Sometimes I have a scoop of vanilla and a scoop of chocolate in my sundaes."

Brooklyn licked her lips.

Oscar paused before he laughed, a rare release for the calm, collected man.

"Just think about it, huh?" Henry sounded so serious and

compassionate.

"I will...*if* you consider something for me." Oscar's tone lightened.

"What's that?" Henry sounded wary.

"Your favorite flavor..." Oscar's taunt was filled with smoke, sexy enough to have Brooklyn shifting behind the hedge.

She balled her fists, prepared to etch a rival's name into her memory so she could hate the cow forever.

"What the hell are you talking about?" Henry scoffed.

"Little Miss Brooklyn?" Oscar singled her out. "Don't act like you haven't been sticking to her like glue. I bet you've seen every single one of her demonstrations in the past year."

"Keeping an eye on our employees, that's all," Henry grumbled.

"Oh, come on." Oscar snorted. "You've given her way more attention than she's warranted. She's never had a single complaint lodged against her, unless it's that she won't spend more time with a guy once he's gotten attached. Hell, you've probably cataloged every freckle on that pert ass by now, haven't you?"

Henry persisted in his excuses, spewing bullshit that had Brooklyn's hair about to burst into flames as she fumed. "Especially with our most advanced hosts, there's always a measure of risk to the guests. Some of the veteran trainers get jaded, reckless..."

Like she felt right then. *No one* insulted her work. Especially not as a way to dodge their own steaming pile of emotional bullshit.

"Fuck you. I'm great at my job." Brooklyn slapped her hands on her latex-clad hips and filled the pathway proudly. A row of delicate Japanese lanterns cast soft light over her bosses' startled expressions. "And I would *never* put one of our visitors in harm's way."

"Ah, Brooklyn." Oscar had the good grace to clear his throat and look as awkward as she'd ever seen him, which was saying something considering the antics of the club. Not even the time the senatorial candidate had sexted a photo of himself in a compromising position, risking the club's shroud of secrecy and his own campaign, had Oscar seemed so uneasy. He shifted on the stone bench, his gaze winging between her and Henry.

"I didn't know espionage was one of your talents." Henry narrowed his eyes. "People don't sneak up on me often."

"There isn't much you've bothered to learn about me." She flexed her fingers on her waist, digging in to stop herself from showing any remorse at his lack of interest.

"Well, let's start now then. What the hell were you doing out there spying on us?" Henry's brows knit as he turned his chocolate gaze on her. "I should—"

"Fire me? Don't bother." Brooklyn couldn't believe the words about to spill from her lips, but her fiery temper flared. Molten emotions ran beneath the sparks of her irritation. He had no idea what he'd stirred within her. She'd had enough disrespect in her life. She wasn't going to take any more. Especially from an arrogant asshole like Henry. Even if he turned her on. Besides, his low opinion of her stung. More than she cared to admit. "If that's what you really think of me and my skills, I quit."

"I was going to say *spank you*. But…" Henry tapped his long index finger on the firm line of his lips, predictably not reacting with equal piss and vinegar. Did he have ice water in his veins?

That had been the problem all along, really. In the two years she'd worked here, he'd never once seemed to give a shit about her or the devotion she had to his adult playground other than as it related to keeping his customers happy. Where he'd chat and mingle with most of the other staff, he'd always been cool and aloof when it came to her. Sure, he watched, but he never applauded along with the rest of the club goers when she finished with a guest and never seemed invested in her success.

Well, fuck that.

Brooklyn spun to leave, catching Oscar's raised brows in her peripheral vision a moment before their greeter whisper-shouted at Henry, "You're not really going to let our best—"

She hadn't made it two strides down the curved paver path before strong fingers landed on her wrist, completely shackling it. When had Henry moved toward her? She hadn't even heard him coming. Maybe both of them were in for some surprises.

"Stop talking, Ozzie." Henry silenced the manager with a single glare, which accompanied his bark.

It wasn't the harsh mandate that had Brooklyn gasping. Instead, the brush of Henry's thumb over her speeding pulse did the trick.

"Well, then. Since you're no longer my employee, I can do what I've been wanting to for a while. Ask you out. Would you rather our first encounter be on familiar ground? Or do you want me to take you away from here right now, somewhere private?" Henry's question flowed over her like smooth whiskey, intoxicating and poisonous if overindulged in.

"What an ego you have!" Brooklyn sneered.

"More like instinct. Don't kiss me back and I'll let you go," he whispered to her as he settled his lips over hers and infused the taste of spice and man into her evening.

Resolute, she kept her mouth firm, unyielding as her spine, which stayed ramrod straight in his grasp. Warm fingers stroked the taut muscles of her back as he continued to persuade her to open for his tongue. The talented muscle prodded the seam of her grimace.

She was hanging tough until she allowed her eyes to

drift open. The up-close-and-personal glimpse of the intensity in Henry's gaze did her in.

Finally, some emotion.

White-hot lust.

Startled, she let out a tiny gasp—enough opportunity for him to weasel his way inside and deepen their kiss. The soft pulls of his mouth as he sucked on her lower lip resonated through her core.

Moisture gathered between her legs, washing away her resistance.

When Henry groaned into her mouth, she realized she had begun to return his advance, meeting him lick for lick with her tongue. Leaning into his secure embrace, she didn't worry once that he'd let her fall when she dedicated herself to stealing a single taste of the forbidden.

And *damn* was it worth it. More decadent than a triple-layer chocolate cake.

The rake of his teeth had her slanting her mouth over his to fuse them more tightly, though such a thing would have been impossible given how he'd wrapped her in his arms as if they were a boa constrictor. She didn't complain about being tucked to his toned body.

Not until he shattered her euphoria and brought her crashing back to reality by separating them enough to give her a glimpse of his shit-eating grin.

"Come on, Brooklyn. Don't deny you feel this chemistry too. I can see your hard nipples through your uniform." Henry singed her with a stare at her chest. Not lewd or degrading, more matter-of-fact, yet lascivious all the same.

She swallowed hard. If she was going to sacrifice her job—the only thing she loved to do, and excelled at in the world—she might as well make it worth it. Then she'd have the satisfaction of walking away from him *and* his club at the end of the night.

Or maybe the weekend.

Something told her they'd need at least that long to work this adrenaline-fueled attraction out of their systems.

Worrying about the rest could come later.

"What will it be?" Henry purred against her neck. "Where do you want me to take you?"

Saying no wasn't an option. Because if nothing else, she was honest with herself. This man was exactly what she'd been craving for two long years. He was the reason she'd denied herself a personal lover outside the realm of her duties.

"Come on, Brooklyn." He didn't give her a chance to spook and change her mind. His thigh pressed between hers and she shivered. "Where will I make you mine?"

If Brooklyn said *Right here*, turn to page 18, *Home Turf (2A)*.

If Brooklyn said *Somewhere else*, turn to page 27, *Let's Jet (2B)*.

Home Turf (2A)

"The club may be your kingdom, but I have my own following here. It's somewhere I'm comfortable." Brooklyn didn't add that it made her feel secure, something she thought she might need to go toe to toe with Henry and survive the walk away—no peeking over her shoulder allowed—when they were finished. After all, part of what made her so at ease had to do with knowing he presided over Underground and all that went on within the club's walls.

Never would he permit one of his hosts, or the guests, to be harmed.

No one dared to cross Henry Emerson.

Except maybe her. This was either the dumbest or best idea she'd ever had.

Besides, if she was about to be banished from the place that had given her ultimate freedom, she insisted on saying good-bye properly.

"I've noticed." Henry put his hand on the small of her back and led her inside. "You're our most requested host. Did you know that?"

"No." She blinked up at him, honestly surprised. "I'm nowhere near as busy as Jeannette or even Cara when we scan through guests' wish lists at the beginning of the night."

"Because Ozzie steers men away if he doesn't think they're a meaningful match for you." Henry escorted her to a service elevator that led to the administrative side of the house. Understated compared to the gothic elegance around them, the plain silver sliding doors encouraged guests to turn their attention elsewhere.

Brooklyn appreciated their solitude. She'd never had a chance to speak with Henry like this. In private. Maybe she could finally get some answers from the enigmatic man who pulled all the strings from afar, even if she hadn't realized it. "You mean if *you* told him they weren't right for me? What was your criteria? All this time I thought the host was free to decide to play or not at their own discretion. I liked making my own decisions. Picking my own pleasures."

She put her hands on her hips, loving the sleek feel of her uniform beneath her fingers. Exiting the car, she followed Henry. They paused while he fiddled with a keypad on a heavy wood-paneled door across the hall from Oscar's office, which she'd been to on numerous occasions. Dumb of her not to realize the unmarked door nearby would belong to Henry.

A quiet beep alerted her to their admission. From inside the darkened interior, Henry murmured, "You've had as much control of your destiny as anyone, Brooklyn. The choice is always yours. You know that. If someone or some activity caught your eye, you were always free to make the first approach. I promise."

Trying not to be awed, she stepped into his lair. Lights slowly came up as an automatic motion sensor brightened the recessed halogens that illuminated a tray ceiling. Half electronics superstore—with monitors galore forming an entire wall—and half old-fashioned gentleman's study with mahogany bookshelves, a globe on a brass stand, and an enormous desk that occupied a third of the space, Henry's headquarters impressed.

It wasn't behind the hulking desk he sat, though. Instead, he led them to a tufted leather couch. The fabric made a funny squeak when she sat on it in her latex uniform.

"How can I be sure of that when I don't know you at all? Why should I think your word is good?" She leaned forward, resting her chin on her fist and her elbow on her knee. Truth be told, her gut screamed that she could rely on Henry.

Still, she questioned her instincts. When dealing with a master player, everything had to be examined in detail. And she recognized him for what he was—an expert at manipulating people. Hell, hadn't he just divulged his deceptions to Oscar? If he could lie to Linley, a woman he clearly respected and adored, he could do the same to her. Right?

"Underground *is* my secret hiding spot. And you know all about that, Brooklyn. You know more about me than you realize." His eyes shone in the glow from the monitors. It had to be lonely to always be on this side of the glass, didn't it? The intermittent flashes caused by people below them passing in front of the cameras reminded her of strobes in the dance hall at the club, where she'd occasionally glimpsed Henry shaking his fine ass to the throbbing bass alongside a throng of other beautiful, if sweaty, people.

Could she live up to his standards? Could they be more alike than different?

She'd whiled away hours in the same pursuit, abandoning herself to the rhythms and pulsating bodies surrounding her on difficult nights. Despite the proximity of all those fellow human beings, she'd never once erased the drifting sensation that had plagued her since she'd lost her family in a tragic head-on collision with a drunk driver.

Funny, she'd forgotten about the aching of her soul since Henry had claimed her hand in his garden. That had to be a record. Ten minutes at least without remembering. Maybe three years of agony was enough for anyone to suffer.

This weekend, she was going to make some major changes.

Starting right now. No more would she wonder about her cryptic boss without demanding answers. She intended to be a hell of a lot more direct. "I heard your whole conversation with Oscar."

He frowned as he glanced over at her. His eyes darkened. She could imagine gathering clouds and storm shutters slamming closed when his whole face went stiff. "Is that why you agreed to tonight?"

"Because you're loaded?" Brooklyn asked herself the

same question and found she didn't have to lie when she said, "No. It's not like I didn't know that already, seeing as you own Underground. Not to mention how well you pay your hosts. Then there's that beast of a car you drive. I don't even know what kind it is, but it screams luxury and speed, neither of which come cheap."

And sex, but she didn't feel the need to pump his head up anymore.

"The club is profitable. Everyone who makes it special deserves a portion of that success." Henry cleared his throat.

Thinking of Underground stole some of Brooklyn's enjoyment. Bantering with him had stimulated her mind as much as her body. She had found something she didn't know she was looking for in the club. And after tonight, that release would be lost to her. There'd be plenty of opportunity to mourn later. Who knew, she might discover something more potent to replace the rush of intimacy with.

Brooklyn refused to ruin her experience with premature regret. Besides, she could relate. Growing up wealthy had made her a target for guys hoping to marry up. It sucked never knowing if you were wanted for you or for what you had.

"Money doesn't mean anything to me." She lightly laid her hand over his where it rested on his ankle, which propped on his other knee. They'd both angled inward so that their legs practically touched.

"Is that why you donated your inheritance to charity?" Henry spoke so calmly she never would have suspected that he'd just hauled a doozy of a skeleton from her closet.

"I kept enough to pay off my student loans and buy a house. Plus I stashed a rainy day fund. More than that seemed greedy." She coughed. "Uh, not that I'm calling you—"

For the first time she could ever recall hearing, he laughed, full and resonant. "I understand. I chair my own philanthropic efforts. How do you think I knew of your impressive donation?"

"Wait. You're not *that* Emerson? From the Emerson Fund? Are you?" This time she didn't simply look at him, she angled her whole body toward the man she'd thought she'd understood. Could he be more than a benefactor of the night, who indulged rich people's fantasies and sowed the seeds of possibilities they couldn't have even imagined on their own? "Holy shit. You *are.*"

"Don't act so surprised." Henry shook her hand free to rub his chest. "Transparency isn't my strong suit, but I didn't think I came off as a total asshole either."

"I didn't say you did." She bit the inside of her lip.

"You didn't have to." This time his chuckle held more bitterness than mirth. "I can tell you think I'm some kind of playboy."

"I'm glad you're not." Genuine relief had her curling closer to him in the intimate space. "Being wrong on occasion doesn't bother me."

"Good. Because I think there's something else you've screwed up." He glanced from beneath his midnight brows at her.

"You could be a little nicer about it. I bet you're capable of manners." Brooklyn poked his side, not even denting his trim torso with the tip of her finger, though she'd jabbed him pretty hard. She swallowed. "Besides, why the sudden interest…in me?"

"That's it exactly. What I'm talking about, I mean. Don't kid yourself, Brooklyn. This day has been coming for quite a while." Henry stared at her with sultry bedroom eyes. A flush resulting from the sexy way he murmured her name washed over her. "I let it go too long. This should have happened a hell of a lot sooner. Like the first time I saw you."

"When I was hired at the club?"

"No. Before that. When you met with the trustees at the

Emerson Fund." He cleared his throat. "See, I own the building where Lane Technology and the Emerson Fund are housed. It was a happy accident that I turned up to inspect Linley's leasehold on the same day she interviewed security specialists. I was curious about her, so I played along. And found I liked her instantly, wanted to help. I accidentally ended up with a position in her organization. Convenient to have a spot smack in between both operations—Lane Technology and Emerson Fund—too. It let me keep an eye on each place at once. Which is how I first caught a glimpse of you. You were delivering your check. I saw you on my security monitor from my office at Lane Technology and I was interested in the heartbroken woman. But I knew I'd be all wrong for a sweet girl like you."

"So I shattered all your misconceptions when I started working at Underground?" She winced. "Is that why you didn't approach me then? You realized I wasn't the innocent you assumed? Are you looking for a princess to complete your empire?"

"Hell, no." He shifted in his seat, enough to make her aware of the uncomfortable bulge in his suit pants. The tailored fit didn't leave much room for his impressive equipment. "That only made me more sure I'd be addicted to you if I ever let myself touch you."

"You were afraid." The revelation shocked her. A man like Henry didn't seem scared of anything. Timid wasn't part of his vocabulary. Still, years as a host had taught her to understand the things her partners didn't tell her outright.

"I'm not proud of that." Henry scrubbed a hand over his jaw before resting his elbow on the arm of the couch. He couldn't have gotten any hotter if he tried. A little susceptibility went a long way toward modifying her opinion of him.

"If it makes you feel better…" She took a deep breath. "I'm kind of worried about the same thing."

"I guess it's all right then." He smiled at her so warmly she began to believe it might be true. "As long as we're hooked on each other, neither one of us has anything to lose."

Brooklyn failed miserably when she attempted to stifle the excitement bubbling up inside her. She decided not to hedge. If he really thought he wanted her, he might as well get used to her occasional impulsiveness. After all, she had quit her job on the spot.

Regret for her lost post at Underground wasn't possible when it meant she'd bought the opportunity to lean forward, climbing to her knees on the couch, and brace her hands on his shoulders. Warm, he singed her through his suit.

Completely relaxed, he allowed her to come to him. So she did.

She gazed into his eyes, which were complemented by all the deep shades of brown in his office, as she eliminated the space between them until only a hairsbreadth remained.

There was only so far you could push a man like Henry, she realized.

With her in range, he struck as quick as a snake in the grass. His hands wound around her neck and held her still as he bridged the tiny gap separating them and sealed his lips on hers. The illicit taste in the garden hadn't been nearly enough to satisfy her craving for him.

Fortunately, he seemed equally starved.

In fact, she wondered if they'd either sit here all night, their tongues dueling for control of their wild make-out session, or if they'd emerge from his office at some point. Frankly, she wouldn't have minded another several weeks of this treatment, his fingers spearing into her hair so he could devour her completely.

Then Henry yanked his head back, panting as he clenched his fists and gritted his teeth, staring at the ceiling.

"That wasn't how I'd planned this to go. If we're not careful…" He lowered his stare to hers ruefully. "This could be over before we start."

"So what exactly do you have in mind?" She canted her head, loving the interconnection of their fingers and the way neither one of them seemed able to quit touching the other.

"Tonight's all about you, Brooklyn." He brushed the pad of his thumb over her lower lip, allowing her to suck on it for a moment before smiling and asking, "You tell me. Where would you like to explore? Not as a host, but as *my* guest?"

She thought of the two levels of the club. Well...there were really three, but the top layer was all fluff—for dinner, drinking, mingling with like-minded friends, and dancing the night away. Without asking, she knew they'd skip this. Things got serious when you descended the grand staircase to the next level, Downstairs.

There you could indulge in a little voyeurism or sexy spanking—among other things—in the lounge before selecting one of the fantasy rooms. There were several she'd avoided with guests, saving them for someday special. *Someone* special.

Henry could be that man.

Or if they were bold enough, they could delve even deeper, into the Basement. Mandatory nudity, she was used to. But would she be able to handle the more extreme pursuits from the passenger seat? Although, there was one room...

Would he be up for letting her turn the tables on him?

Tough decisions. She tapped her lip with one of her blood-red manicured nails.

Sexy times could be had in either place, though there was a playfulness in Downstairs that didn't reach the depths of the dungeon below it. She took her time, considering her options, thrilled that he'd given her the power to decide.

Then again, depending on what she chose, the reins could wind up in either of their hands. What did she want?

A wild, sweaty fling or something darker. More

serious…

Either would be unforgettable.

A deep sigh expanded her chest, drawing Henry's full attention to her breasts. His blatant appreciation gave her the courage to make a decision—to go all out and claim this chance to make a fantasy come true with her dream man.

"I'm going to go with…"

If Brooklyn said *Downstairs*, turn to page 38, *Going Down (3A)*.

If Brooklyn said the *Basement,* turn to page 50, *Going Way Down (3B)*.

Let's Jet (2B)

"Take me away from here. I want this time to be ours. Alone." Brooklyn didn't intend to share this new side of Henry with their colleagues or the regular guests. It was too much pressure, with the multitude of eyes that would focus on them—a new, temporary couple. Tongues would wag. Especially if she disappeared after their liaison burned out.

This opportunity to live her dreams had cost her enough to justify a private show.

Besides, all she cared about was what Henry thought, not the rest of Underground. Or the world for that matter. Most people would call her a lunatic for giving in to his demands. For sacrificing her career.

Long ago she'd learned to depend on her gut, which aimed unwaveringly in Henry's direction like a pointer dog standing at attention on a duck hunt.

Or was it part of her slightly lower than her navel leading the charge right now?

"I'm glad you feel that way." Henry clasped her hand and looked over his shoulder toward Oscar, who smiled. "Have my jet ready in thirty minutes, including luggage for us both, with essentials for the entire weekend."

"What? I can't—" Brooklyn objected.

"You were working a full shift until Monday, staying in the staff quarters here. No different now except you'll spend the time with me instead." Henry's swollen mouth tipped up at the corners. "I promise I'll make it worth your while."

She didn't doubt that for a second.

Before she could find some other excuse to renege on the wild deal she'd made, Henry tugged her along the path toward the subterranean garage that sheltered his ridiculous ride. She had no idea what the make and model of the thing was. But she knew what it had done to her the few times she'd seen him roll up to the curb in it. Sleek lines and low growling sounds painted a clear picture of power and luxury knotted into a giant wad of sex appeal.

It suited him well.

Henry handed Brooklyn into the passenger seat of his car—though the term seemed too mundane for this machine—squeezing her fingers before he released them. The scent of leather and speed flared her nostrils as she buckled in, prepared for the ride of a lifetime. Hell, when had this gone from a first date to something that felt like a metamorphic experience?

The instant she'd agreed to this madness.

Because Henry Emerson would never be ordinary. He took everything to the extreme. Even his courting, it would appear. Tenacity only added to his addictive qualities. Heady and exciting, he revved her engine as surely as he started the one that would carry them from the safe haven she'd known these past two years.

Brooklyn stared as her escort on this insane adventure stalked around the hood of the car then curled his impossibly long frame beside her, taking his place behind controls better suited to a fighter pilot than a driver. Which reminded her...

"Where are we going?" She tipped her head at him, trying not to focus on how strong and graceful his hand looked on the gear shifter or how in control the other seemed as it guided the steering wheel. They spiraled up the cement ramp that led from the depths housing some of the city's most elite vehicles—their owners inside Underground, kicking off a night of debauchery.

"It's up to you." He smirked at her.

"Then why do I feel like I'm being dragged to the bat cave or something?" The loose strands of hair around her face tickled her forehead as they fluttered in the breeze caused by her sigh.

"I think you have it backward. Underground is my secret hiding spot. And you know all about that, Brooklyn. You know more about me than you realize." His eyes shone in the glare from oncoming headlights and the streetlamps they zoomed past. Though it wasn't completely dark yet, the intermittent flashes reminded her of strobes in the dance hall at the club, where she'd occasionally glimpsed Henry shaking his fine ass to the throbbing bass alongside a throng of other beautiful, if sweaty, people.

Could she live up to his standards?

She'd whiled away hours in the same pursuit, abandoning herself to the rhythms and pulsating bodies surrounding her on lonely nights. Despite the proximity of all those fellow human beings, she'd never once erased the drifting sensation that had plagued her since she'd lost her family in a tragic head-on collision with a drunk driver.

Funny, she'd forgotten about the aching of her soul since Henry had claimed her hand in his garden. That had to be a record. Ten minutes at least without remembering. Maybe three years of agony was enough for anyone to suffer.

This weekend she was going to make some major changes.

Starting right now. No more would she wonder about her cryptic boss without demanding answers. She intended to be a hell of a lot more direct from now on. "I heard your whole conversation with Oscar."

He frowned as he glanced over at her. His eyes darkened. She could imagine gathering clouds and storm shutters slamming closed when his whole face went stiff. "Is that why you came with me?"

"Because you're loaded?" Brooklyn asked herself the same question and found she didn't have to lie when she said, "No. It's not like I didn't know that already, seeing as you own Underground. Not to mention how well you pay your hosts. Oh, yeah, and the fact that you have your own freaking jet."

"The club is profitable. Everyone who makes it special

deserves a portion of that success." Henry cleared his throat. Thinking of Underground stole some of her enjoyment. She had found something she didn't know she was looking for in the club. And now that release was lost to her. There'd be plenty of opportunity to mourn later though. Who knew, she might discover something more potent to replace the rush of intimacy with.

Brooklyn refused to ruin her weekend with premature regret. Besides, she could relate. Growing up wealthy had made her a target for guys hoping to marry up. It sucked never knowing if you were wanted for you or for what you had.

"Money doesn't mean anything to me." She lightly laid her hand over his on the shifter.

"Is that why you donated your inheritance to charity?" Henry spoke so calmly she never would have suspected that he'd just hauled a doozy of a skeleton from her closet.

"I kept enough to pay off my student loans and buy a house. Plus I stashed a rainy day fund. More than that seemed greedy." She coughed. "Uh, not that I'm calling you—"

For the first time she could ever recall hearing, he laughed, full and resonant. "I understand. I chair my own philanthropic efforts. How do you think I knew of your impressive donation?"

"Wait. You're not *that* Emerson? From the Emerson Fund? Are you?" This time she didn't simply look at him, she angled her whole body toward the man she'd thought she'd understood. Could he be more than a benefactor of the night who indulged rich people's fantasies and sowed the seeds of possibilities they couldn't have even imagined on their own? "Holy shit. You *are.*"

"Don't act so surprised." Henry shook her hand free to rub his chest. "Transparency isn't my strong suit, but I didn't think I came off as a total asshole either."

"I didn't say you did." She bit the inside of her lip.

"You didn't have to." This time his chuckle held more bitterness than mirth. "I can tell you think I'm some kind of playboy."

"I'm glad you're not." Genuine relief had her curling closer to him in the intimate space. "Being wrong on occasion doesn't bother me."

"Good. Because I think there's something else you've screwed up." He glanced from beneath his midnight brows at her.

"You could be a little nicer about it. I bet you're capable of manners." Brooklyn poked his side, not even denting his trim torso with the tip of her finger, though she'd jabbed him pretty hard. She swallowed. "Besides, why the sudden interest...in me?"

"That's it exactly. What I'm talking about, I mean. Don't kid yourself, Brooklyn. This day has been coming for quite a while." Henry glanced at her from the corner of his bedroom eyes before returning his full focus to the road. He steered the car effortlessly as the flush resulting from the sexy way he murmured her name washed over her. "I let it go too long. This should have happened a hell of a lot sooner. Like the first time I saw you."

"When I was hired at the club?"

"No. Before that. When you met with the trustees at the Emerson Fund." He cleared his throat. "See, I own the building where Lane Technology and the Emerson Fund are housed. It was a happy accident that I turned up to inspect Linley's leasehold on the same day she interviewed security specialists. I was curious about her, so I played along. And found I liked her instantly, wanted to help. I accidentally ended up with a position in her organization. Convenient to have a spot smack in between both operations—Lane Technology and Emerson Fund—too. It let me keep an eye on each place at once. Which is how I first caught a glimpse of you. You were delivering your check. I saw you on my security monitor from my office at Lane Technology and I was interested in the heartbroken woman. But I knew I'd be all wrong for a sweet girl like you."

"So I shattered all your misconceptions when I started working at Underground?" She winced. "Is that why you didn't approach me then? You realized I wasn't the innocent you assumed?"

"Hell, no." He shifted in his seat, enough to make her aware of the uncomfortable bulge in his suit pants. The tailored fit didn't leave much room for his impressive equipment. "That only made me more sure I'd be addicted to you if I ever let myself touch you."

"You were afraid." Somehow it surprised her. A man like Henry didn't seem scared of anything. Timid wasn't part of his vocabulary. Still, years as a host had taught her to understand the things her partners didn't tell her outright.

"I'm not proud of that." Henry scrubbed a hand over his jaw before resting his elbow on the top of the door, against the window. He couldn't have gotten any hotter if he tried. A little susceptibility went a long way toward modifying her opinion of him.

"If it makes you feel better…" She took a deep breath. "I'm kind of worried about the same thing."

Before he could answer, Henry turned into a well-lit gate. A guardhouse stood on one side. In the distance, Brooklyn spotted the air traffic control tower of the city's main airport. Personal jets lined up behind the fence topped with razor wire. She'd never been to the private section of the facility before.

This sure as hell beat taking the shuttle to the main terminal and plodding through security.

"Good evening, Mr. Emerson." The discretely armed man leaned into the open window. "Your garage has been unlocked. The crew is set to arrive within the next five minutes. Have a safe flight."

"Thanks, Leo." They rolled forward into the gathering evening. High-powered halogens mixed with the dregs of sunlight filtering through the sparse cloud cover. They highlighted the scruff on Henry's cheeks and the fine lines around his smile when he pulled into the open bay and cut the engine.

His hands caressed the leather steering wheel for a moment before he reached for the door handle. Brooklyn didn't care to sit there and wait for him to retrieve her, so she climbed out of the deep bucket seat on her own and nearly bumped into Henry, who steadied her with his long fingers on her elbow.

"Come on." He surprised her by leaning in to kiss her cheek. "Let me show you around, get comfortable before the crew joins us."

"How much could there be to see?" She assumed his private plane wasn't exactly the equivalent of the jumbo jets that occasionally rattled the window panes of her house.

"Plenty." His wicked smile clued her in.

Depending on how the weekend went, she figured she stood a good chance at joining the mile-high club on the return trip. It might be a nice parting gift to them both.

Brooklyn's smile slipped a bit thinking of the only place this lark could lead them.

"You're not afraid of flying, are you?" Henry didn't rush her, though the incessant stroking of his thumb on the inside of her upper arm nearly drove her mad. In a good way.

"No." She didn't suppress the happy memories that flooded her. "It's been a while, but I always enjoyed tagging along with my dad on business trips."

"Perfect." He steered her into a building that could have been any office in the world, complete with a tidy yet sterile waiting room, until they popped out of the other end of the hallway onto the tarmac.

"Wow." From here, his jet looked plenty big enough. A row of windows dotted the structure, guaranteeing there was room for more than a handful of guests. She'd guess it was more than regional transportation, capable of transatlantic flights. Transpacific, maybe.

She should have saved her awe.

When he led her up the stairs and through the open door, she only had a moment to wonder which of his minions had prepped the plane before the crew arrived. Then all menial thoughts flew from her mind as she took in the polished wood and rich leather of the interior. Everything gleamed yet remained inviting. Comfortable without sacrificing style or lavishness.

A reflection of Henry in every way she could imagine.

"You can stow your bag here." He led her to a cubby that hung above the deep couch before turning toward the bar and filling two tumblers with a nutty brown liquid. Whiskey, she smelled a moment later.

"Your drink of choice?" Brooklyn sipped, letting the alcohol wash over her tongue. Nothing but the best here either.

"Same as yours." He clinked their glasses together. "At least according to the bartender at Underground."

She still couldn't believe he knew so much about her.

"There's a restroom at the rear if you'd like to freshen up before we take off. Maybe change out of your uniform, if you'd be more comfortable." Henry leaned against the spalted maple, polishing off the remaining finger of liquid in his glass. The bob of his Adam's apple entranced her.

Clearing her throat, Brooklyn decided a splash of brisk water on her face might work wonders. Something had to cool her down soon or she'd make a fool of herself before they'd even lifted off. "Thanks."

She headed for the door he'd indicated only to realize it wasn't exclusively a washroom. Beyond the threshold, a full suite waited. Deep blues and burgundy declared it a man's zone. The immense bed was more than even Henry's tall frame and broad shoulders would require.

Quickly, she took care of business, including fixing her hair and wishing she routinely wore more makeup. There wasn't much point at Underground. Between sweating and various other activities, she usually smudged it off before she'd been there an hour.

What did Henry think of that? He couldn't mind too much, since he'd practically ordered her out with him tonight. After all, the hosts were free to do as they pleased. Show guests a good time and enjoy themselves as much as possible. They were never forced to partner with someone, but were merely paid to enjoy the environment as they saw fit.

Brooklyn couldn't deny arousal flowed through her now, both because she'd been prepared for a weekend of no-strings debauchery at the club and more because of the twist her life had taken. Surely Henry felt it too.

Flipping through a few outfits that hung from the shower rod, she opted for simple. Not that she needed to keep her uniform on as some kind of armor, but…well, she found herself unwilling to part with the familiar just yet. Still, she admired some of the selections. Light and airy dresses, or jeans and a pretty lavender top with a deep *V* neckline. Something completely unlike what he'd seen her in before. Would he like the more casual part of her too?

Maybe. But this was who she was. The Underground uniform wouldn't be hers much longer, so she chose not to part with it so soon. Would he get her message?

All doubt fled when she emerged from the restroom and found him lounging on the couch, scanning her from head to toe. There was no mistaking the gleam in his eyes.

"Come here." He patted his lap instead of the cushion beside him.

"Don't expect me to protest like some innocent maiden, okay?" She nibbled on her lower lip as she sank into his hold.

"Stop worrying." He kissed the tiny wound she'd made. "I admire your passion. I only want to share it."

Then there was no more talking because they both leaned in to each other. She wound her arms around his shoulders and buried her hands in his thick hair as she'd imagined doing so many times before.

With a growl, he pressed his lips over hers. The hard length of his erection dug into her hip as he tightened his embrace, drawing her closer to his torso. She didn't resist, allowing him to meld them from waist to shoulders as she perched across his lap, her legs extending onto the couch.

His hands roamed up and down her spine, supporting her even as he enflamed her. She devoured him in return. Soon his tongue fluttered along her lips, teasing until they parted on a gasp.

Without pausing for permission, he invaded.

Henry melted every shred of resistance she possessed. Why wouldn't she keep kissing him, taking their exchange deeper, when he made her feel so alive?

For the first time in years, excitement pulsed from every pore. She couldn't wait for the next sip of his mouth or the massage of his tongue against hers. Completely devoted to their lip lock, she didn't hear the crew board the aircraft.

Judging by Henry's jerk beneath her when the captain cleared his throat, neither had he.

Brooklyn backed away and leaned her forehead on Henry's. She laughed softly at the dazed look in his eyes. At least she wasn't the only one suffering. The husky rasp of her amusement startled her. It didn't even sound familiar. Already Henry had taken her places no one else had.

When he licked his lips and took a deep breath, as if preparing for another scorching kiss, the captain said, "Excuse me."

Brooklyn glanced over at the man wearing a crisp blue uniform in time to catch his wince.

The captain looked to Henry from the threshold of the cockpit, his face stony, as if he hadn't busted them making out like teenagers. "I'm sorry, sir. I need to submit our flight plan. Where are we headed?"

Henry tucked a strand of hair behind Brooklyn's ear, acting like it was perfectly normal to have a woman cradled on his lap while speaking to his pilot. Maybe it was for him, though she didn't think so.

"If it were my choice, I'd pick Paris. You deserve the most romantic city in the world." He kissed the tip of her nose. "Then again, the beach is never a bad place either. Private, too, on my island. Skinny-dipping is fair game. All day—weekend—long if you prefer."

"Are you saying it's up to me?" Brooklyn stilled, her eyes widening. It wasn't every day Henry Emerson gave someone else even the illusion of control.

"To me it only matters that I'm with you." He surprised her with his sweet talking, mostly because it seemed genuine. "Anywhere you go, Brooklyn, I'll follow."

"Wow. I don't know what to say—" She rarely found herself speechless.

"Tell the man where to fly us." Henry jerked his chin toward the pilot, who waited patiently. "Quickly. I have plans."

If Brooklyn said *Paris, please*, turn to page 66, *City of Love (3C)*.

If Brooklyn said *I hope you brought sunscreen*, turn to page 78, *Henry's Paradise (3D)*.

Going Down (3A)

"Let's start Downstairs. We can always work our way deeper." Brooklyn stopped herself before implying they'd play another night. She wished it were true, but Henry had made no mention of his intentions beyond this one wicked evening. Then again, they could hit two levels in a single session. If anyone was capable of double dipping, it'd be the man she straddled on this super comfortable couch.

When had that happened?

Virile and ultimately confident, he held her waist and allowed her to dictate their direction.

"Fine. We'll head out in a moment. First, get rid of that uniform." He steepled his fingers, kicked back like this was some seedy casting call and she the starlet. For some reason that didn't bother her much.

Brooklyn narrowed her eyes. Shedding her clothes would be the same as sacrificing her identity at Underground. She supposed she'd already done that, though.

As if he sensed the wound she'd self inflicted, Henry reached out and squeezed her thigh. "I don't want anyone making a mistake tonight. I'd like it to be clear that you're out of play. Mine. Only mine tonight."

"I wouldn't want you to have to bruise those knuckles again like the time Kage Gunner put his paws on Regina after she'd told him she wasn't interested." Brooklyn looked away. The raw power he'd exuded as he'd laid the bastard out had stuck with her. "I always thought you had a thing for her after that."

"Just instinct. My job, really." Henry growled. "And that asshole did more than let his hands wander across her ass. They also dipped into a few ladies' purses in the cloakroom on the main level. I was waiting for more evidence to bust him, but that was the final straw. Can't say I didn't enjoy it either."

"I didn't know that." She winced.

"Guess I'm starting to understand why you never approached me, despite this chemistry." Henry seemed ready to tug her into his lap once more. But if he did, they'd never investigate the possibilities lurking below them. "I waited for you to come to me, you know."

Brooklyn darted from his grasp without an answer. None came to her as she considered the lost time they might have wasted. How could she have known?

Thankful for the tinted glass of his floor to ceiling windows, which overlooked the atrium on the top floor of the club, she squirmed and wiggled in the patented shimmy she conducted every night after she'd finished partying at Underground. It began with hopping around to remove her boots and ended with a twist of her hips as she peeled the skintight latex over her curviest parts. Every motion jiggled her boobs, which were bare and exposed. "I swear you designed this getup precisely for the show I'm putting on now."

"It *is* very entertaining." Henry adjusted himself as discreetly as possible given the thick bulge of his package. "I swear it was a happy accident. The uniform does wonderful things to a woman's body, enhances something already amazingly beautiful. Although in your case, I think I prefer you naked. Sometimes nature gets things perfect all on its own."

His appreciative stare scanned her from head to toe. He spent equal time gazing into her eyes as he did assessing her shaved mound. Both appraisals triggered reactions in her, one gooey and one spicy. They pleased her equally.

So she strutted to Henry, as if drawn by a magnetic force she had no hope of escaping. No desire to either.

"Want me to take the edge off for you, sweetheart?" he asked. "Or will being horny help you keep your brave face on when we make our entrance in the club?"

The thought of being on Henry's arm took her breath away. Her knees wobbled.

He reached out to steady her, grinning as he gathered her close once more.

With his hands on her hips, he drew her forward until he nuzzled her mound. Breathing deeply, he practically purred at the scent of her arousal. Inspired by him.

"Going straight for the kill, huh?" Brooklyn tried not to be so affected. Yeah, right.

"Would you prefer traditional romance?" He gazed up at her, though he didn't stop placing soft kisses below her belly button or massaging her ass once he had her in his clutches. "We could back up, start again, go somewhere else..."

"No." She regained some of her composure. Burying her fingers in his hair, she aimed his mouth a tad lower, on level with her pussy.

"Thank God." He flashed a wolfish grin at her before taking matters into his own hands, literally.

Henry lifted her and tumbled her to the couch. Still fully clothed in his five thousand dollar suit, he slithered between her legs. There was something undeniably taboo about being completely nude in his fancy office while his silk tie brushed her soaking pussy.

"I'll never get any work done in here again," he lamented. "Every time I sit at my desk, I'll be remembering you laid out like a centerfold. Do you have any idea how beautiful you are, Brooklyn?"

She shrugged, more interested in how he made her feel with the teasing swirls of his fingers through her slit. How could he talk like nothing was going on when everything in her focused on his caresses?

Henry tamed her even as he inflamed her.

"Please," she begged, though she didn't know what she was asking for, unless it was some kind of relief.

He growled as he pounced, burying his face in her folds

without gradual introductions. Sliding his arms beneath her, he cupped her shoulders and pulled her tight to his talented mouth. If his fingers had provoked, his lips delivered. Light flicks alternated with deep sucks and quick twirls of his tongue.

Brooklyn pinched her nipples, alleviating some of the ache building there as they puckered with each burst of pleasure he gifted her with. Before she could fully register all the rapture flooding her system, he introduced two fingers into her flexing sheath.

With something to hug, something to squeeze, she found herself hovering on the brink of orgasm in record time.

Henry didn't give her the option of lingering. As if he sensed her susceptibility, he began to twist his wrist, screwing his hand deeper even as he scissored his fingers within her. That alone would have been enough to make her come, but he didn't stop there. Next he began to pump into her with a slow, steady motion that forced her to struggle for breath and arch.

Finally, he changed his oral recipe from an even mixture of ingredients to an all sucking diet. The pressure on her clit was the last straw.

Brooklyn surrendered to orgasm. Her pussy contracted. She feared for Henry's poor fingers, which might now be broken. The climax surprised her.

It was quick.

It was furious.

It was amazingly good.

Like a bite-sized candy bar. Or a stolen morsel from someone else's plate. The intense release gave her a taste of what waited ahead for them. It whetted her appetite, leaving her hungry for more.

For a moment they both stayed entwined, catching their breath and waiting for the world to settle into place around their heaving chests. Brooklyn would swear Henry had enjoyed his treatment nearly as much as she had. She wouldn't have taken him for the sort of man to relish going down on his woman, but he clearly did. Faking gusto like that would have been impossible.

Even now, he licked his lips as if he might make a second course of her.

"I think we should go. Now." She rose, tugging him to his feet beside her. Next time they tangoed, she needed to feel him inside her, fucking her so well she wouldn't regret one second of their encounter.

"One last thing." Henry crossed to his desk and opened the top drawer, withdrawing something from a box. He palmed whatever it was and returned with measured strides.

"What's that?" Brooklyn pointed as she studied his fist and the odd expression on his face.

"I hope you don't think this is too…forward." He kind of stumbled on the old-fashioned term, making her even more curious. A tongue-tied Henry Emerson? Impossible. "Linley told me you'd admired it a while ago when you were shopping. It was going to be a present for—"

He shook his head, stopping himself.

She might have pressed him on the matter if he hadn't rotated his wrist so his fingers faced up then uncurled, revealing a teardrop blue opal pendant she'd forced herself to walk away from when she couldn't justify the splurge. It wasn't ostentatious. Unique styling and quality craftsmanship impressed her more than gaudiness.

Before she thought better of it, her fingertip traced the platinum setting.

"You may strut through Underground naked, but you'll wear this." He didn't take no for an answer—not that she objected—when he unclasped the chain and swooped behind her, brushing her hair aside to fasten his token around her neck.

People here were used to seeing men and women in

collars. They would know what the necklace meant. So did she.

And yet, she didn't find herself the least bit interested in unstaking his claim.

"Thank you for not arguing." He kissed her neck beside the metal encircling her throat. "It brings me a lot of pleasure to see you smile like that. And to know I had some part in it."

"You're doing a pretty great job of making me happy." She tipped her head up for another kiss.

Henry surprised her again by multitasking, slipping his jacket off his shoulders, unknotting his tie, then tearing through the buttons of his shirt. He shucked his suit pants. Soon he was standing in front of her in not much more than his probably one-of-a-kind Jaeger-LeCoultre watch. She recognized the logo from her father's pride and joy, a relic she had found it impossible to part with.

"I thought we were going Downstairs?" Taking a step back, she admired his chiseled chest and abdomen.

"We are." Standing there in boxer briefs, he was sexier than the model she'd seen on a bus wrap traveling through the city last week. Obviously it was the man that made the underwear. "But I need to change first."

His tight ass flexed as he crossed to a closet beside the couch he'd so recently dazzled her on. From inside it, he withdrew a fistful of leather and metal rings.

Henry donned the harness as if it were second nature. The fierce straps highlighted his muscles, especially his biceps when he added a cuff to each arm. He whipped the cotton from his ass, leaving her to admire the paler tone of his buns for a moment. Last, he carefully removed his watch and set it on a shelf at the top of the locker.

Then he committed a travesty against all women by covering up male perfection with tight leather pants, even if they left nothing to the imagination. Okay, those might not be so bad after all.

Barefoot, he stalked toward her, then past to the door. Holding it wide, he ushered her through and to the elevator. He punched the button three times.

"In a hurry?" Brooklyn had finally found her tongue again.

"Hell, yes." He clamped her hand in his and stepped into the mirrored car.

She had to admit they looked great together. Both tall and fit. Henry must have thought so too if his hum of approval was anything to go on.

"Get ready to blow their socks off, sweetheart." He kissed her cheek then put his shoulders back and chest out, as if proud to be seen with her. Able to say the same, Brooklyn stood straighter.

"I'm only concerned about your opinion." The truth slipped from her before she remembered to fake nonchalance.

"And vice versa."

Then the doors slid open. The familiar salacious landscape spread out before them. A host greeted them and promised drinks were on the way without bothering to ask what they wanted. Well trained, all the regulars' favorite orders had been committed to memory.

A rush of whispers cleared the way for them, chatter traveling faster than the sight of the unlikely pairing. By the time the crowd had parted enough to allow Brooklyn and Henry to join the main gathering in the Downstairs lounge, all talk had ceased.

Brooklyn couldn't ever recall it being so damn quiet.

Masters had stopped spanking their partners mid swing, the woman giving her guy a blowjob in the center of the area stuttered then paused with a mouthful of cock, and several people froze with their wine glasses halfway to their lips.

Henry didn't address the spectators with an overblown speech. His reaction, though simple, said it all. He lifted their joined hands above their heads, proclaiming their matchup for all to see. The symbol of his ownership, temporary though it might be, glittered around her neck.

Spontaneous applause exploded through the entire level. New faces and old friends clapped as they witnessed the bond pulsing between her and Henry. At least it felt like it did to her.

Additional guests and staff alike poured through the curtain that blocked the view from the upper level and peeked through the railing of the spiral staircase to the Basement to see what all the fuss was about, then stayed to add their whistles and cheers to the roar of popular sentiment.

Horrified, Brooklyn felt a tear gather then roll down her cheek. She hadn't expected the approval of their community to mean so damn much.

Her emotion didn't go unnoticed by Henry. Attuned to her every move, every breath, he faced her and offered an indulgent smile. He whispered, "Yeah, me too."

Then he kissed her again. This time the ovation of the gathering didn't register beyond the focus he claimed from her. Nothing mattered except the flash of heat he inspired. It was a miracle she didn't climb him right there.

Hell, she might have if he hadn't nipped her lower lip before goading her. "I dare you to put on a show for your fans."

"They're cheering for you," she countered.

"I don't think so." The firm set of his mouth made it clear that arguing would be futile.

"What did you have in mind?" She blinked up at him slowly, her lids weighing at least as much as a dump truck.

"How about a lap dance?" A grin came over his face, so fierce it held a hint of grimace.

"Last time I checked, Underground wasn't that kind of club." Could she do that? Was she graceful enough, seductive enough? If there weren't so many people watching, she might not have worried. But she knew that Henry wouldn't be the only one judging her performance.

Henry chuckled. "I want to watch you move. More, I want to see every man in this place jealous of what I'm about to do."

"Aren't you used to people coveting your life? How is this any different?" She truly wondered.

"I've never had something as valuable as you before." The sincerity in his tone hit her square in the chest with as much force as the strongman at the fair taking a sledgehammer to one of those midway games. Lights and bells sounded in her heart while she figured she'd won the best prize imaginable, though a giant stuffed pink elephant would have been pretty cool, too.

Before she could chicken out, she settled her hands on his shoulders and shoved, knocking him into the chair behind him. Designed for a multitude of uses, it was sturdy, not even shaking beneath his muscled weight when he landed in the leather seat and laid his hands on the carved wooden arms like a king on his throne.

"Music!" he barked.

Within seconds, the melody of a smoky jazz song wound around them. It was easy to imagine herself as the kind of entertainer who'd start out sprawled on a grand piano in a sequined cocktail dress and end up spinning tassels on equally flashy pasties as a burlesque number concluded.

So she went with it.

Gyrating to the beat, she shimmied and dipped, teasing Henry with a face full of her cleavage. The room seemed to appreciate the rear view just as much. When the man beneath her reached out, she smacked his hands. "No touching. You know the rules."

"Jesus." His head *thunked* against the headrest of his massive chair. "I should have known you'd be too damn good at this."

"Who me?" She posed with her knees bent, angled to the side and her hands folded beneath her chin, the picture of innocence before she ran the tip of her index finger down his nose.

"Hell, yes. You. Vixen." He sucked the digit into his mouth, reminding them both of how he'd given her pussy similar treatment not long ago. And would again. Soon, if she was lucky.

Her best chance was to drive him insane with lust until he couldn't resist a moment longer.

Brooklyn thanked her merciless yoga instructor when she put one foot on Henry's shoulder. Leaning on it, she allowed herself to spread completely before him, her back leg far enough away to make her practically do the splits for his enjoyment. Even a farsighted man would have had no trouble making out every detail of her pussy from that intimate distance.

"Damn," he groaned. His fingers twitched on the armrest as though he might crack, violate her hands-off mandate, and test the moist paradise she laid out before him.

Retracting her foot before he dared, because certainly she'd end up begging him to take her right then and there, she strutted around him in a circle, teasing his chest and ruffling his hair from behind.

Several *whoops* resounded from men—and maybe a couple of women, too—nearby as she displayed her goods to best effect.

When she made it back to Henry's prime viewing area, she turned up the heat, grinding her pelvis in time to the sultry beat.

As the song peaked, Brooklyn leapt. She planted her feet on either side of Henry's thighs and dropped low over his crotch. Twerking in his lap, she adored the twitch of his cock against her ass through the leather of his pants.

"Fuck her!" Someone shouted when the song faded into

nothing.

Henry could have easily accomplished the deed in this position. All she'd have to do was open his fly, lift up a bit, and help him slip inside. Tempted, she waited for his directive.

"I plan to," Henry responded to the heckler, though he never once looked away from her. He kissed her neck, short-circuiting her brain, before saying, "Come on, sweetheart. It's time to get serious. Pick a room before things get out of control. Another minute and I'm not going to stop. I want to share this with you. Alone."

She scrambled to her feet, grateful for his hand, which gripped her elbow and kept her from sinking to the floor again when her jellied legs wobbled. Attempting to speak, twice, only resulted in two simple words. "This way."

He followed the incline of her chin. The invisible pointer led them toward a bank of doors. Each one featured a plaque that hinted at the delights found within. On top was either a red or green light. Though Brooklyn was sure a single raised finger from Henry would clear any of the spaces, it didn't seem fair to interrupt the couples already playing inside.

Fortunately, the two areas she'd had in mind both were clear.

She headed in their direction. Unsure of her final destination, she stutter-stepped, then drew up short in the hallway.

"So where are you taking me?" He peered between the rooms on either side of where they'd stopped.

The two she was most interested in happened to be side by side.

"I haven't quite decided." She eyed them both.

"But you never pick these when you entertain guests." Henry raised a brow at her.

"I know. I've been saving them." Brooklyn blushed. Both required a hell of a lot of trust. Another thing she never gave a casual playmate. Crap.

"So which will it be?" He squeezed her hand. "If you're wondering, either of them sound fan-fucking-tastic to me. Spanking and sex swings are two of my favorite ways to play."

She bit her lip and considered, wishing she could have them both. Maybe she could if they hadn't thoroughly worn each other out after their session.

"Come on, sweetheart. Pick one. Do you want the spanking room? Or would you rather try out the swing?"

If Brooklyn said *I've been naughty*, turn to page 90, *Spank Me, Henry (4A)*.

If Brooklyn said *I've always liked playgrounds*, turn to page 99, *Sex Swing (4B)*.

Going Way Down (3B)

"Why pull our punches? I'm ready for anything. Take me to the Basement tonight." Brooklyn stopped herself before implying they'd play another time. She wished it were true, but Henry had made no mention of his intentions beyond this sole wicked evening. Then again, they could hit two levels in a single session. If anyone was capable of double dipping, it'd be the man she straddled on this super comfortable couch.

When had that happened?

Virile and ultimately confident, he held her waist and allowed her to dictate their direction.

"Fine. We'll head out in a moment. First, get rid of that uniform." He steepled his fingers, kicked back like this was some seedy casting call and she the starlet. For some reason that didn't bother her much.

Brooklyn narrowed her eyes. Shedding her clothes would be the same as sacrificing her identity at Underground. She supposed she'd already done that, though.

As if he sensed the wound she'd self inflicted, Henry reached out and squeezed her thigh. "I don't want anyone making a mistake tonight. I'd like it to be clear that you're out of play. Mine. Only mine, tonight."

"I wouldn't want you to have to bruise those knuckles again like the time Kage Gunner put his paws on Regina after she'd told him she wasn't interested." Brooklyn looked away. The raw power he'd exuded as he'd laid the bastard out had stuck with her. "I always thought you had a thing for her after that."

"Just instinct. My job, really." Henry growled. "And that asshole did more than let his hands wander across her ass. They also dipped into a few ladies' purses in the cloakroom on the main level. I was waiting for more evidence to bust him, but that was the final straw. Can't say I didn't enjoy it either."

"I didn't know that." She winced.

"Guess I'm starting to understand why you never approached me, despite this chemistry." Henry seemed ready to tug her into his lap once more. But if he did, they'd never investigate the possibilities lurking below them. "I waited for you to come to me, you know."

Brooklyn darted from his grasp without an answer. None came to her as she considered the lost time they might have wasted. How could she have guessed he lusted after her, too?

Thankful for the tinted glass of his floor to ceiling windows, which overlooked the atrium on the top floor of the club, she squirmed and wiggled in the patented shimmy she conducted every night after she'd finished partying at Underground. It began with hopping around to remove her boots and ended with a twist of her hips as she peeled the skintight latex over her curviest parts. Every motion jiggled her boobs, which were bare and exposed. "I swear you designed this getup precisely for the show I'm putting on now."

"It *is* very entertaining." Henry adjusted himself as discreetly as possible given the thick bulge of his package. "I swear it was a happy accident. The uniform does wonderful things to a woman's body, enhances something already amazingly beautiful. Although in your case, I think I prefer you naked. Sometimes nature gets things perfect all on its own."

His appreciative stare scanned her from head to toe. He spent as much time gazing into her eyes as he did assessing her shaved mound. Both appraisals triggered reactions in her, one gooey and one spicy. They pleased her equally.

So she strutted to Henry, as if drawn by a magnetic force she had no hope of escaping. No desire to either.

"Want me to take the edge off for you, sweetheart?" he asked. "Or will being horny help you keep your brave face on when we make our entrance in the club?"

The thought of being on Henry's arm took her breath away. Her knees wobbled.

He reached out to steady her, grinning as he gathered her close once more. With his hands on her hips, he drew her forward until he nuzzled her mound. Breathing deeply, he practically purred at the scent of her arousal. Inspired by him.

"Going straight for the kill, huh?" Brooklyn tried not to be so affected. Yeah, right.

"Would you prefer traditional romance?" He gazed up at her, though he didn't stop placing soft kisses below her belly button or massaging her ass once he had her in his clutches. "We could back up, start again, go somewhere else..."

"No." She regained some of her composure. Burying her fingers in his hair, she aimed his mouth a tad lower, on level with her pussy.

"Thank God." He flashed a wolfish grin at her before taking matters into his own hands, literally.

Henry lifted her and tumbled her to the couch. Still fully clothed in his five thousand dollar suit, he slithered between her legs. There was something undeniably taboo about being completely nude in his fancy office while his silk tie brushed her soaking pussy.

"I'll never get any work done in here again," he lamented. "Every time I sit at my desk I'll be remembering you like this. Do you have any idea how beautiful you are, Brooklyn?"

She shrugged, more interested in how he made her feel with the teasing swirls of his fingers through her slit. How could he talk like nothing was going on when everything in her focused on his caresses?

Henry tamed her even as he inflamed her.

"Please," she begged, though she didn't know what she was asking for, unless it was some kind of relief.

He growled as he pounced, burying his face in her folds without gradual introductions. Sliding his arms beneath her, he cupped her shoulders and pulled her tight to his talented mouth. If his fingers had provoked, his lips delivered.

Light flicks alternated with deep sucks and quick twirls of his tongue.

Brooklyn pinched her nipples, trying to alleviate some of the ache building there as they puckered with each burst of pleasure he gifted her with. Before she could fully register all the rapture flooding her system, he introduced two fingers into her flexing sheath.

With something to hug, something to squeeze, she found herself hovering on the brink of orgasm in record time.

Henry didn't give her the option of lingering. As if he sensed her susceptibility, he began to twist his wrist, screwing his hand deeper even as he scissored his fingers within her. That alone would have been enough to make her come, but he didn't stop there. Next he began to pump into her with a slow and steady motion that forced her to struggle for breath and arch.

Finally, he changed his oral recipe from an even mixture of ingredients to an all sucking diet. The pressure on her clit was the last straw.

Brooklyn surrendered to orgasm. Her pussy contracted. She feared for Henry's poor fingers, which might now be broken. The climax surprised her.

It was quick.

It was furious.

It was amazingly good.

Like a bite-sized candy bar. Or a stolen morsel from someone else's plate. The intense release gave her a taste of what waited ahead for them. It whetted her appetite and had her hungry for more.

For a moment they both stayed entwined, catching their breath and waiting for the world to settle into place around their heaving chests. Brooklyn would swear Henry had enjoyed his treatment nearly as much as she had. She wouldn't have taken him for the sort of man to relish going down on his woman, but he clearly did. Faking gusto like that would have been impossible.

Even now, he licked his lips as if he might make a second course of her.

"I think we should go. Now." She rose, tugging him to his feet beside her. Next time they tangoed, she needed to feel him inside her, fucking her so well she wouldn't regret one second of their encounter.

"One last thing." Henry crossed to his desk and opened the top drawer, withdrawing something from a box. He palmed whatever it was and returned with measured strides.

"What's that?" Brooklyn pointed as she studied his fist and the odd expression on his face.

"I hope you don't think this is too…forward." He kind of stumbled on the old-fashioned term, making her even more curious. A tongue-tied Henry Emerson? Impossible. "Linley told me you'd admired it a while ago when you were shopping. It was going to be a present for—"

He shook his head, stopping himself.

She might have pressed him on the matter if he hadn't rotated his wrist so his fingers faced up then uncurled, revealing a teardrop blue opal pendant she'd forced herself to walk away from when she couldn't justify the splurge. It wasn't ostentatious. Unique styling and quality craftsmanship impressed her more than pure gaudiness.

Before she thought better of it, her fingertip traced the platinum setting.

"You may strut through Underground naked, but you'll wear this." He didn't take no for an answer—not that she objected—when he unclasped the chain and swooped behind her, brushing her hair aside to fasten his token around her neck.

People here were used to seeing men and women in collars. They would know what the necklace meant. So did she.

And yet, she didn't find herself the least bit interested in unstaking his claim.

"Thank you for not arguing." He kissed her neck beside the metal encircling her throat. "It brings me a lot of pleasure to see you smile like that. And to know I had some part in it."

"You're doing a pretty great job of making me happy." She tipped her head up for another kiss.

Henry surprised her again by multitasking, slipping his jacket off his shoulders then tearing through the buttons of his shirt. He shucked his suit pants. Soon he was standing in front of her in not much more than his probably one-of-a-kind Jaeger-LeCoultre watch. She recognized the logo from her father's pride and joy, a relic she had found it impossible to part with.

"I thought we were going to the Basement?" Taking a step back, she admired his chiseled chest and abdomen.

"We are." Standing there in boxer briefs, he was sexier than the model she'd seen on a bus wrap traveling through the city last week. Maybe it was the man that made the underwear. "But I need to change first. Even I'm not exempt from the *no clothing* rule."

His tight ass flexed as he crossed to a closet beside the couch he'd so recently dazzled her on. From inside it, he withdrew a fistful of leather and metal rings.

Henry donned the harness as if it were second nature. The fierce straps highlighted his muscles, especially his biceps when he added a cuff to each arm. He whipped the cotton from his ass, leaving her to admire the paler tone of his buns. Last, he carefully removed his watch and set it on a shelf at the top of the locker.

When he pivoted, she bit the inside of her cheek to keep her tongue from lolling out of her gaping mouth or from gasping like a virgin on prom night. To see him nude stole her breath, this time as all times. More, because he intended to do something about the attraction they shared. She was easily the luckiest bitch in the entire city tonight. Probably the entire country. Hell, possibly the world.

It wasn't only his cock, which hung heavy between his thighs even half hard. Henry Emerson, complete package, would make any woman swoon. Her included. Barefoot, he stalked toward her, then past to the door. Holding it wide, he ushered her through and to the elevator. He punched the button three times.

"In a hurry?" Brooklyn had finally found her tongue again.

"Hell, yes." He clamped her hand in his and stepped into the mirrored car.

She had to admit they looked great together. Both tall and fit. Henry must have thought so too if his hum of approval was anything to go on.

"Get ready to blow their socks off, sweetheart." He kissed her cheek then stood straighter, his shoulders back and chest out, as if proud to be seen with her. She could certainly say the same.

"I'm only concerned about your opinion." The truth slipped from her before she remembered to fake nonchalance.

"And vice versa."

Then the doors slid open. The familiar salacious landscape spread out before them. Dark walls blended with black painted apparatuses scattered in the corners. Couches and thick rugs made lounging…or more…convenient. Comfortable for enjoying the scenes developing despite the early hour. Later in the night—early morning, really—things would get progressively more interesting until the last guest left, sated and exhausted.

A host greeted them and promised drinks were on the

way without bothering to ask what they wanted. Well trained, all the regulars' favorite orders had been committed to memory. That went twice for the boss's preferences.

A rush of whispers cleared the way for them, chatter traveling faster than the sight of the unlikely pairing. By the time the crowd had parted enough to allow Brooklyn and Henry to join the main gathering in the Basement lounge, all talk had ceased.

Brooklyn couldn't ever recall it being so damn quiet.

Masters had stopped flogging their submissives mid swing, the woman dripping wax on her chained man spilled some of the hot liquid on the floor, and a guy getting blown by two women squeaked when they must have lost concentration and caught him with their teeth on a rather sensitive place.

Henry didn't address the spectators with an overblown speech. His reaction, though simple, said it all. He lifted their joined hands above their heads, proclaiming their matchup for all to see. The symbol of his ownership, temporary though it might be, glittered around her neck.

Spontaneous applause exploded through the entire level. New faces and old friends clapped as they witnessed the bond pulsing between her and Henry. At least it felt like it did to her.

Additional guests and staff alike peeked through the railing of the spiral staircase that descended from Downstairs to see what all the fuss was about, then stayed to add their whistles and cheers to the roar of popular sentiment.

Horrified, Brooklyn felt a tear gather then roll down her cheek. She hadn't expected the approval of their community to mean so damn much.

Her emotion didn't go unnoticed by Henry. Attuned to her every move, every breath, he faced her and offered an indulgent smile. He whispered, "Yeah, me too."

Then he kissed her again. This time the ovation of the

gathering didn't register beyond the focus he claimed from her. Nothing mattered except the flash of heat he inspired. It was a miracle she didn't climb him right there.

Hell, she might have if he hadn't nipped her lower lip before goading her. "I dare you to put on a show for them."

"What did you have in mind?" She blinked up at him slowly, her lids weighing at least as much as a dump truck.

"How about you come for them?" A grin so fierce it held a hint of grimace came over his face. Henry leaned close to whisper in her ear. "Every man in this place is jealous of what I'm about to do. Maybe we should let them have a little fun."

"Aren't you used to people coveting your life? How is this any different?" She truly wondered.

"I've never had something as valuable as you before." The sincerity in his tone hit her square in the chest with as much force as the strongman at the fair taking a sledgehammer to one of those midway games. Lights and bells sounded in her heart while she figured she'd won the best prize imaginable, though a giant stuffed pink elephant would have been pretty cool too.

"So you want *them* to touch me?" She couldn't reconcile his statement with what he hinted at. "How does that make sense?"

"I want to give *you* as much pleasure as possible, even if that means recruiting some help." Henry grimaced. "I'm man enough to admit I can't do as good of a job as half a dozen guys working together. You're worth sucking up my jealousy. At least for a little while. That's as much as I can stand right now."

"More than I expected." Brooklyn surprised him by going onto her tiptoes to lay a kiss on his lips. The *whoops* from the patrons around them brought her to her senses before they dropped and started fucking right there on the floor.

Barely.

"Here's how we'll play." That sensual smile returned.
"Hold out as long as you can. I dare you. Put on a good show
and I'll let you decide which playroom we move our private
party to afterward."

Her head fell back, exposing her neck, which Henry
swooped in to rake his teeth over. "You know I won't last."

"I guess I didn't do a very good job in my office then,
did I?" He frowned.

"More like I can't get enough of you. One clitoral
orgasm isn't going to cut it tonight." She didn't bother to
pretend otherwise.

"Well it's not like you can overdose on climaxes." He
slapped her ass to get her moving in the right direction,
toward the gang of guests milling about. "So have fun."

When she glanced down, the sight of his erection nearly
had her calling off this delay. After all, what she really
craved was him. But the sight of the pre-come glistening at
the tip convinced her not to intervene when he so obviously
enjoyed their game.

"If you insist." She smiled then strode into the throng
with more confidence than she actually possessed given the
lack of her uniform and the corresponding void left in her
identity. No longer was she one of the elite.

Or maybe she was something untouchable. Henry's.

Without being told, she climbed onto a low platform.
Nothing like a night of firsts. She gulped as she lowered
herself until she stretched out on her back with her neck
resting against the half circle cut in a board. Leather trim
ensured it cradled her comfortably. The placement left her
head in the center of four low wooden walls that extended a
few inches above her face.

"You don't have to go that far." Henry murmured to her,
though she barely heard him above the rumble of the
onlookers, who commented to their neighbors in hushed

tones about their good luck. He crouched beside her, staring into her eyes as if to gauge her seriousness. Or maybe her arousal.

The head box took a lot of guts. It wasn't something that got used all the time. When she didn't immediately deny a change of venue, he offered her options. "If you want to rest on the exam table over there instead, that's fine by me. Or even the couch."

"Like this." She shook her head then forced her body to relax, her fingers uncurling and resting, splayed on the leather of the platform surface. "Hurry."

"You're amazing." He kissed her hard then twisted to the side to grab the top half of the box. It was identical, though mirrored from the part she'd laid on. When he put it over her then clamped it to its base, she was locked in darkness.

And yet her body remained displayed for everyone else to see and enjoy as Henry allowed. Like a stockade, but more extreme, the device isolated her and trapped her with her own thoughts while simultaneously exposing her body.

Worse, she knew that while she couldn't see the crowd, a night vision camera embedded in the planks boxing her in allowed them to witness her every reaction, projected onto the wall behind her cage. Safety dictated the inclusion of the device.

Titillation was merely a side benefit for the guests.

The sudden change left her in complete blackness despite the light leaking in the loose fit around her neck. Her eyes, unadjusted, couldn't even make out the grain of the box top no more than three inches in front of her face. The echo of her own ragged breaths haunted her.

When a warm hand squeezed her thigh, she shrieked.

"Brooklyn? Are you okay?" Henry sounded more serious than she'd ever heard him. "Answer me. Now. Or you're coming out."

"No!" She flailed, though she missed him entirely with her grasping hands. "I mean, yes. I'm fine. Don't quit on me."

"Please," she mouthed. And he must have seen it on the screen. He patted her leg then caressed the length of her hip and torso before claiming her fingers.

"I'm going to hang on to you the whole time, okay?" He promised her a safety net. "If you get scared or want to stop, let go."

"Never." Let him read what he liked into that.

Neither of them had a chance to speculate though, because Henry must have given his consent. A softer, smaller hand surrounded her ankle. Then a cooler one fondled her right breast. And then there were too many to count.

People groped her from her shoulders to her toes.

With anonymity, it was easy to imagine all of them were Henry. She knew their touches were an extension of his desire, a gift he hoped she'd enjoy. Refusing to disappoint him, she allowed herself to be spurred by the jumble of sensations.

A pinch here, a rub there.

A squeeze. A tap.

Touches everywhere.

Someone even jiggled her breast.

When she spread her legs, begging for someone to rub the maddening buzz beginning to escalate in her clit, a collective murmur of approval filtered into the head box.

"Are you sure, Brooklyn?" Henry increased his grip on her fingers, and she mimicked the pressure. "I have a time in mind. A certain number of minutes. If you want to pick your pleasure for the rest of the evening, you have to outlast it. Let the rapture build before you surrender so easily. You're supposed to be an expert."

"Fuck you." She hoped he caught her wink onscreen.

He chuckled, though someone slapped her inner thigh

hard enough to sting. Based on his position holding her hand and a sixth sense, she speculated it had been him. Somehow he felt different than all the others. Inflamed her more.

Though it could have been her imagination, she hoped not.

Brooklyn tried recalling the name of every state in alphabetical order, but it was no use.

The constant petting of a dozen or more men—and perhaps a few women, if she didn't mistake their sultry handling—couldn't be ignored. Especially not when mouths joined the effort. Wet and steamy, they dragged along her flesh—kissing, licking, nipping. The tips of her breasts were popular, as were her toes, for some reason.

The shuffling of participants as they jockeyed for access, sometimes knocking into her or pressing harder than intended, only riled her further. Someone finally answered the begging she hadn't realized had escaped her mind and become a near shout.

Several people massaged her mound, her inner thighs, and finally her pussy.

Fingers wormed into her. Different sizes—lengths and girths.

Though she shook, she kept true to her promise and smothered Henry's hand with hers. At least one of them. The pattern drawn around her clit with the pad of a thumb felt awfully familiar, similar to the one his tongue had painted there not a half hour earlier.

Moans began to escalate, making her wonder what kind of orgy might be breaking out around her. Knowing she'd done that, turned them on, had power. She rocked her hips upward, begging for more. Though nearly every inch of her was claimed by a questing hand, it wasn't quite enough.

Until Henry called to her. The circles interspersed with taps on her clit paused and a pet across her belly had her insides clenching. "Hey, gorgeous. Time. You can come, free and clear."

The instant strange hands were knocked aside by the one familiar touch, she allowed all the various sensations to overwhelm her inhibitions. Uncaring if they saw the astonished expression on her face, never mind the juices flowing from her overstimulated pussy, Brooklyn yielded to their attention. Even if he hadn't given her permission, she would have conceded defeat.

There was no choice in the matter.

The roving hands and mouths catapulted her into ecstasy.

She came so hard her heels drummed on the leather-topped platform. Guests, and maybe other hosts, embraced her. They soothed her with light strokes over her goose bumped skin until the riot of sensation passed.

Over time, the clamps of her pussy turned to pulses and then finally a liquid serenity she knew would be short lived. As soon as she saw Henry, and—hopefully—the approval on his face, the emptiness in her pussy would demand to be filled.

Finally.

Sure enough, the hands left her one by one with lingering farewell caresses.

"Close your eyes. This may be bright at first." Henry reintroduced her to the world around them when he lifted the lid of her heavenly prison.

Brooklyn blinked up at him. Coming into focus, his face reflected everything she'd expected and more. A reverence she'd never imagined smoldered in his eyes. Without words, he told her how beautiful he thought she was, a magnificence that was more than skin deep. She knew because she felt the same about him.

That he'd given her a chance to find a new place within her...

Well, tonight was priceless.

Worth every sacrifice.

Brooklyn raised her arms to him and he obliged by scooping her up. He carried her away from the wide-eyed stares of the crowd he'd used to please her. Out of the limelight, they shared a deep, lingering kiss.

"Where do you want to go next?" Henry asked when he came up for air. He jerked his chin at the wall of doors. Each one contained a fantasy darker and more alluring than the one before, though his introduction would be hard to top.

"It's really up to me?"

"Did you think I'd change my mind? You earned your pick." His charming grin seemed both out of place and right at home in the den of sensuality he'd constructed.

"What if I want you to kneel at *my* feet?" At first she intended it to be a joke, but the more she thought about directing the rest of the evening, the more attractive the ex-lark became. If she could only have him this once, taking it all her way wasn't the worst thing possible.

Then again, as tempting as it might be to put that harness hugging his chest to good use, there was one room she'd been dying to investigate since she'd started here. Yet never before had she trusted someone enough for one of the most extreme adventures offered at Underground.

With anyone else, an unsupervised visit to the chamber wouldn't have been permitted. Hell, even with her and Henry, Oscar was likely to monitor if not intercede.

She peeked into the far corner, which not many were brave enough to enter.

"That?" Henry rubbed his knuckles over his five o'clock shadow. "Water bondage? Christ, Brooklyn. That's...sexy. And diving right into the deep end. Pun intended."

If she let him bind her—something she rarely permitted anyone to do—instead of the other way around, added stimuli specific to that room would elevate the experience to the fringes of her comfort zone.

Breath control, for one. The dunk tank in the room took center stage.

She'd peeked in the open door once, before the club opened. She'd imagined what it might be like to sink below the surface, peering out of the glass at the man holding her very life in his hands. A shiver ran through her from her toes up, until even her hair stood on end.

Henry pinched her nipple hard enough to trigger an echo in her pussy.

"So what will it be?" He smirked. "Who's in charge tonight?"

Both of them understood it would be an ultimate power exchange.

Brooklyn considered a few moments more, then sighed happily. Either way, him allowing her to make the decision granted her all the authority. She knew what she wanted. And she couldn't believe she'd finally found the right man to explore this fantasy with.

If Brooklyn said *You're not my boss anymore*, turn to page 120, *Femdom (4D)*.

If Brooklyn said *I hope you like mermaids*, turn to page 108, *Water Bondage (4C)*.

City of Love (3C)

"Paris, please." Brooklyn couldn't believe she refrained from giggling when she issued the request to the captain, though she figured anywhere they traveled together would be as close as she got to utopia.

"Yes ma'am. I assume you won't be requiring in-flight service today, sir?" The knitting of the captain's fingers in front of him made it seem like he tried his damnedest not to raise his brows at Henry.

"Well, I wouldn't say that." Henry earned a smack on his shoulder from Brooklyn. He only laughed as he continued, "But we don't need a flight attendant."

The captain tipped his hat then turned into the cockpit, closing the door securely behind him and the copilot she noticed inside. Brooklyn thought she caught the ghost of his smile right before he slipped from view. She didn't blame him.

Hell, she might have been grinning like the Cheshire cat herself.

"Have you ever been before?" Henry asked.

"Only if you count the dozen travel guides I've stockpiled or the French lessons I took last summer, or maybe the fascination I have with bistro cooking." She tried not to sound pathetic, but the evidence was pretty damning. Paris ranked high on her bucket list.

So did sex with Henry.

"I'm glad to be going with you then." He caressed the nape of her neck, pressing until some of the muscles there liquefied.

"I'd rather you were coming with me first." She didn't pretend to be subtle. Why start now? "It's a pretty long flight, isn't it?"

"We'll have plenty of time after takeoff to…explore a little if you want."

"Why not a lot?" She tilted her head when something in his voice made her curious.

"I'm the kind of guy who saves my favorite chocolate in the box for last. I unwrap my Christmas presents slowly instead of tearing the paper." He ran his finger down her nose. "When you've got everything a man could want, it's rare to experience...*anticipation*...like this."

"Rich people problems, huh?" Brooklyn chuckled.

"Is that a deal breaker for you?" He didn't deny her jab hit close to home.

"I like sex. A lot." She didn't blush or even glance away from his eyes when she confessed what he already knew. "With you, I'll probably enjoy it a whole lot more."

"I can't go all night without a taste of you at least." Henry pinched the bridge of his nose for a moment. "Don't laugh, but I'd kind of like our first time to be special."

"Isn't that supposed to be my line?" Brooklyn couldn't believe it possible that Henry Emerson had a shy bone in his body. Maybe it was simply inexperience. Debonair he had down pat. Romantic, however, could be as new for him as it was for her.

"If I did anything the traditional way." He cupped her shoulders in his big hands and made sure she was paying close attention. "That isn't my style. You're what I prefer."

"So what's the holdup?" Brooklyn squirmed on his lap enough to torture them both. "I saw that bed back there. It might not be the biggest I've ever done it in, but it certainly looked lush. Lots of pillows. I like that."

"Is that some kind of euphemism?" Henry narrowed his eyes.

"Nope." Brooklyn trailed her fingers down his sculpted chest, then his abs. "I haven't gotten a good enough feel to make any of those kinds of comparisons. Yet. Hiding something?"

She could tell enough to know he didn't have to.

Besides, tales from his past lovers were legendary around Underground.

"Screw that." He might have protested more vehemently except they began to taxi just then, so he buckled them in instead of defending his manhood.

They accelerated down the runway and launched into the air, leaving her insides jellied, or maybe Henry had something to do with that. As soon as they got the signal from the captain that they could move about the cabin, Henry stood in a rush, scooping Brooklyn into his arms as if she weighed nothing. Sure, she worked out plenty, but she'd always been the tallest of all her friends. Good thing Henry towered above most men or she'd be doomed to sacrifice her fetish for high heels.

"I'd rather fuck you." Why bother pulling her punches at this point?

"An appetizer for now." Henry toted her to the bedroom and kicked the door shut. He maneuvered through the tight spaces with the grace of a jungle cat, never once so much as banging her elbow.

"I've never been a fan of diets." Brooklyn did her best not to pout.

"I'll make it worth your wait." He silenced her with a kiss that scattered all her objections. All she could focus on was the heat of their lips dancing as he set her on the bed.

Henry didn't break their contact for a moment as he shucked his suit jacket then toed off his expensive shoes, which were polished so thoroughly they'd gleamed even in the partial shade and failing sun of his garden.

Speeding the process along, she unknotted his tie, hoping he'd find better uses for the silk later. Soon he was standing in front of her in only his probably one-of-a-kind Jaeger-LeCoultre watch. She recognized the logo from her father's pride and joy, a relic she had found it impossible to part with.

Propped on her elbows in a mountain of down, she stared at Henry's finely chiseled muscles. He could have been a statue in one of Paris's world-famous museums.

An instant classic, she thought.

Brooklyn's gaze scanned him from his slightly furred chest to his washboard abs. She licked her lips as she studied his long, thick erection, which hardened by the second. His legs enthralled her with their length, strength, and the fine curve of his calves. Still, she came back to his groin. The bulkiness developing there as she appraised him required her to cup her breast to ease some of the heaviness that settled in her chest.

"Thanks." His smug pose, arms crossed, feet spread, only enhanced his sex appeal.

Brooklyn reached behind her for a pillow to launch in his direction.

He fended it off easily then pounced, rolling her to her stomach and straddling her before she could protest. Not that she would have.

Henry unzipped her uniform in record time. Hell, it usually took her a few contortions and shimmies to work her way free of the latex. A master of seduction, he peeled it off, kissed her between her shoulder blades then flipped her over before she'd even finished being grateful for freedom from the restricting garb.

The thick shaft of his cock weighed heavy on her belly when he hovered over her, placing a kiss on the tip of each of her breasts before wandering up to reclaim her mouth. Though she wished their increasingly frantic parries of tongue and lips could satisfy her completely, she needed more.

Henry chose right then to rip his mouth away. He shot her a steamy stare before sinking lower, spreading her legs around his torso as he nibbled a path toward her core. Without wasting a moment, he scented the air as if getting high on her arousal, then dove into the moist flesh between her legs.

If the skill of his tongue hadn't been obvious when he'd kissed the shit out of her, there was no denying his talents when he employed them to flick his deft muscle against her clit, circling, tapping, and fluttering in an assault of pleasure guaranteed to curl her toes in record time.

Before she could warn him, she felt herself spiraling out of control, something that never happened at Underground. Sex was sex. Pleasurable, sure. An epic release of tension and worry. Freedom from her daily life. Not this terrifying flight toward the unknown.

Brooklyn heard herself whimper.

"It's okay." Henry lifted his head long enough to reassure her. "I've got you. Let me see how beautiful you are when you come. For me."

Had he watched her climax for others? Probably, as not all areas of Underground guaranteed privacy.

Henry embedded two fingers in her clenching pussy. Whatever nerves he pressed, they were definitely the right ones to light up her entire body like an old-fashioned switchboard when gossip flew across town.

Brooklyn unraveled in his hands. She stared into his warm, dilated eyes as she surrendered to his wishes, which matched hers exactly. Orgasm washed over her, drowning her in relief that was chased by renewed desire when he pumped his hand between her legs, drawing out the ecstasy.

Only this time, she wanted to taste him, too.

When she reached for his hip, he caught on quickly, rotating without abandoning her pussy until he spanned her again, this time with his knees on either side of her head. She didn't have to strain her neck reaching for his cock. The tip prodded her lips, glossing them with his pre-come.

Brooklyn sucked him into her mouth, savoring the flavor of man and heat. She relished the groan he surrendered and the thrill of the resulting vibration on her pussy. Once more, he dedicated himself to lifting her higher up the corkscrew of rapture she hadn't quite slid all the way down after her dizzying climax.

Brooklyn wondered how long they could torture each other like this.

Not more than a few minutes at first. It seemed Henry was every bit as eager as she was for relief. Maybe then they could focus on getting to know each other, when there was room for rational thought in between her instincts, which screamed at her to bend over for the man dominating her so naturally.

She employed every fancy move she'd mastered in the past few years to lave his cock so well he'd never forget her or this night. At least she hoped he wouldn't be able to.

Still he managed to get her off a handful of times before she felt him tensing above her.

Brooklyn grabbed Henry's ass and dug her fingernails into the knotted muscles there, dragging him forward until she'd captured every inch of his impressive shaft, even though it meant he was buried in her throat. And when she swallowed around him, she had the satisfaction of hearing his primal growl and a half-hearted warning.

A few pulls of her mouth later and he was pouring his release into her. She showed her appreciation for the dazzling pleasure he'd gifted her with by joining him, satisfied she'd made her point when he kissed her inner thighs between whispered curses and praise.

Henry softened. He withdrew despite her gentled suckling, then gathered her to his chest where he wrapped them both in fine linens and her in his arms.

"Sleep, Brooklyn." He nuzzled the crown of her head with his chin. "It'll be morning when we arrive. And there's so much I want to show you."

Though she attempted to stifle her yawn and vote for

more bedroom games, Brooklyn found herself obeying his gravelly commands. Her eyes drifted shut and she burrowed into the warmth and security of his hold.

Doing something she hadn't ever before, she fell asleep in a man's embrace, looking forward to waking in exactly the same place.

Hell, they never even had to get off the plane. This had already been the trip of a lifetime.

Brooklyn wasn't usually the hand-holding type. Oddly, she found herself glad Henry refused to release her when she shook his fingers slightly as they prepared to descend the jet's staircase.

Dressed in one of the gorgeous watercolor silk sundresses he'd supplied, along with more clothes than she probably had in her closet at home, she felt like a fairy tale had swooped in and replaced her life. If only he'd caved to her pawing this morning, she could die happy.

Instead, he'd shown her how well he could use a showerhead to pleasure her again—and, *oops*, again—before buckling her in for their landing. She'd been too weak to protest their lopsided affair.

With one hand she held the rail, dizzied by the steps she took downward, partially because she scanned the horizon for the peak of the Eiffel Tower, and partially because of Henry's effect on her. Still he clenched her fingers in his, despite the awkward twist of his arm behind his back.

Spotting the tippy top of the city's most recognizable landmark from the ground made it feel more real than it had when she'd glimpsed the crisscrossing beams of its skeleton through the porthole-shaped window of Henry's plane. With the rose-hued sky of early morning behind the structure, she couldn't imagine many things more romantic.

Unless it was the man escorting her through the Charles de Gaulle International Airport's terminal with his hand spanning the small of her back. The implication of possession went straight to her core, setting her pulse somewhere between frantic and pre-heart attack.

Dazzled, she blinked at him as they stepped into the dappled morning sun. The scent of fresh croissants wafted from a pâtisserie across the street, nearly causing her to drool. At least she told herself it was the delicacy and not the man beside her.

"Come on. I know the perfect café for breakfast. I could eat a dozen servings of the wild berry and honey crepes." He hailed a cab as he took note of her preferences. "How do you feel about scouting out the attractions in the city, since it's your first time? Or would you rather shop? Or settle in to a hotel?"

Though the last option tempted her, she couldn't pass up the opportunity to tour Paris.

"Treat it like it's vacation boot camp, Henry." She grinned. "I want to see it all."

With him.

"All right. Tell me when you're ready to cry uncle." He smiled as he registered her enthusiasm.

But she didn't quit after they climbed the minarets at Notre Dame for a close-up of its famous gargoyles, or when they took the river cruise down the Seine and he narrated their tour, knowledgeable about more than just the major monuments. Not even when they stopped at Sainte-Chapelle to see the endless stained glass then walked to the Panthéon, or next to the Tuileries Garden. Hell, he even kept up with her when the concierge at the Louvre swore they'd never make it in time to see the Mona Lisa. She'd sprinted past the Winged Victory of Samothrace and flew down the endless gallery to catch a glimpse of da Vinci's smirking lady.

"What do you think?" Henry waited for her to examine the portrait.

"It's…okay." As much as she wanted to love it, she couldn't help but think she'd jogged past more beautiful, if less known, works in her mad dash.

To her surprise, Henry laughed. "My thoughts exactly. Meh. Want to see my favorite?"

As the curators began striding from the far reaches—practically arm in arm, sweeping out guests—Henry strolled along as if he owned the place, pointing out at least a dozen pieces of art she truly adored.

Finally, they erupted from the glass pyramid in the courtyard above the museum. Henry asked if she was ready to quit. "No way. We haven't seen the Eiffel Tower yet."

He pointed. "It's right there."

Brooklyn tapped his abdomen with the back of her hand. His six-pack didn't budge and had her distracted for a split second. "I'm sorry. Am I keeping you from something you'd rather be doing?"

He kissed her knuckles. "I was only teasing. I've already made reservations at Le Jules Verne in the tower. If we hurry, we can ride to the top first."

"What if there's a line?" Brooklyn checked her antique watch.

He only smiled.

When they arrived, Brooklyn began to realize Henry might be even wealthier than she imagined. He was greeted by name at the box office and a woman in uniform led them to the front of the miles-long snake of people for their own private ride to the summit.

Henry stood behind her with his arms looped around her waist as they ascended. She couldn't decide which was more mesmerizing—the city unfolding before them or the reflection of them bundled together in the glass of the elevator car. For sure, when she peeked at Henry, he only had eyes for her.

When at last they stood near the edge together, Brooklyn wondered if it were possible to count the infinite twinkling lights in the early evening. They looked like fireflies. Or maybe stars. And she couldn't stop herself from making a wish.

That this night could last forever.

Right then, Henry swooped in and whispered against her parted lips. "I don't know what you're thinking about, but I hope it's me. That look...*Christ*."

He kissed her, this time with both more passion and more tenderness than he had in the jet the night before. As she stood on her tiptoes for another taste of him, she knew dinner might contain amazing courses...but she was ready to devour him for dessert.

Stuffed and exhausted, yet oddly energized, Brooklyn followed Henry toward the arched Metro sign leading to the Champ de Mars station. Before they could be washed into the entrance by the stream of people they had become part of, he stopped. Pedestrians split around them like water flowing past a boulder.

"What's wrong?" She reached up to cup his cheek in her hand. The bold curve of his jaw fit perfectly there.

"I'm not sure where we're going." He blinked at her a few times.

"There's a map at the bottom of the stairs." She could barely see the edge of it from here.

"That's not what I meant. I've always felt like there are two sides to me, Brooklyn." He held her hands tight in his as if begging her to understand. "The Henry Emerson everyone presumes they know, and the one who lives Underground. Maybe a third sliver belongs to Linley. It was amazing to have a relationship with no expectations beyond friendship and doing a good job. Horrible too, not to share the real me. You're the first woman I've met who knows both halves yet seems compatible with each."

"The same goes for me, Henry." She squeezed his fingers. "I've been living in shadows. You don't make me explain why I need what I do. Never once have you questioned me about being a host."

"Because I get it." He drew her to him and braced her shoulders in his hands. "It makes you whole. It fills the emptiness."

"Yeah, it does," she whispered before nuzzling his neck.

"So which half wins tonight, Brook?" Henry hugged her to him. "It can be different next time. But for now...do we belong on top of the world or do you want to see what makes it tick?"

For a moment, her mind looped around the promise of a future rendezvous. *Next time*, he'd said. That seemed most important. He had a reputation for never taking the same partner twice. Could she truly be special to him?

"Which one have you taken fewer women to?" An uncommon urge to have her lover to herself came over her. She was afraid it might be a permanent craving with Henry.

"Each are the same. I've never shared either place." He stared into her eyes as if their gazes were drawn by force. "With anyone. You're different, Brooklyn. You mean something *more* to me. I know it's ridiculous to make promises at this point..."

"So don't." She leaned in and covered his mouth with hers before he could say something they'd both regret later— him when he came to his senses and her when she allowed herself to believe the romantic spell this witchy city had cast on them right before he broke her heart.

Brooklyn had been abandoned enough already.

Moving on, alone again, after a weekend of pretending to be in a relationship was going to kill her.

"I have a couple of places I'd like you to see." Henry's earnest stare had her leaning even closer. "One makes you feel like you're practically in heaven."

"The Eiffel Tower again?" Brooklyn couldn't help her obsession with the monument especially after their amazing feast and the even more spectacular kiss they'd shared there.

"No, somewhere better. You'll never forget the view, including the lit-up tower. It's worth the hundreds of stairs to get there, I promise. I'll even give you a massage considering all the walking we did today. The other is… Well, maybe we should save that for later."

"No, tell me." She at least wanted to decide. The fact that he would let her spoke volumes. He trusted her choice, something she knew not many people could say.

"It's down there." He cast his gaze toward their feet.

Brooklyn recalled the PBS special she'd seen on the labyrinth of tunnels that snaked beneath the City of Lights. The City of *Love*. Some were catacombs, filled with bones and who knew what else. Others comprised a network of waterways. Still more acted as secret passages used by politicians, thieves and…well, people like Henry, she supposed.

"Both places seem appropriate. With you I feel like I'm flying. And still so grounded." She looked to the sky then to the cracks in the sidewalk that managed to appear charming instead of shabby. "So maybe we could do both eventually?"

"Of course." He nodded. "But tonight? Where should we start our adventure, Brooklyn? At the top of the world or in the heart of it?"

If Brooklyn said *Top of the World*, turn to page *135, Arc Top (4E)*.

If Brooklyn said *Heart of It*, turn to page *147, Labyrinth (4F)*.

Henry's Paradise (3D)

"I'm going to have to go with fun in the sun. Take us to Henry's Paradise, please." Brooklyn couldn't believe she refrained from giggling when she issued the request to the captain, though she figured anywhere they traveled together would be as close as she got to utopia.

"Yes, ma'am. I assume you won't be requiring in-flight service today, sir?" The knitting of his fingers in front of him made it seem like he tried his damnedest not to raise his brows at Henry.

"Well, I wouldn't say that." Henry earned a smack on his shoulder from Brooklyn. He only laughed as he continued, "But we don't need a flight attendant."

The captain tipped his hat then turned into the cockpit, closing the door securely behind him and the copilot she spotted inside. Brooklyn thought she caught the ghost of his smile right before he slipped from view. She didn't blame him.

Hell, she might have been grinning like the Cheshire cat herself.

"Have you ever been to the Caribbean?" Henry asked.

"Only if you count the dozen travel guides I've stockpiled or the SCUBA lessons I took last summer, or maybe the fascination I have with cooking seafood." She tried not to sound pathetic, but the evidence was pretty damning. Trying out island life ranked high on her bucket list.

So did sex with Henry.

"I'm glad to be going with you then." He caressed the nape of her neck, pressing until some of the muscles there liquefied.

"I'd rather you were coming with me first." She didn't pretend to be subtle. Why start now? "It's a pretty long flight, isn't it?"

"We'll have plenty of time after takeoff to…explore a little if you want."

"Why not a lot?" She tilted her head when something in his voice made her curious.

"I'm the kind of guy who saves my favorite chocolate in the box for last. I unwrap my Christmas presents slowly instead of tearing the paper." He ran his finger down her nose. "When you've got everything a man could want, it's rare to experience…*anticipation*…like this."

"Rich people problems, huh?" Brooklyn chuckled.

"Is that a deal breaker for you?" He didn't deny her jab hit close to home.

"I like sex. A lot." She didn't blush or even glance away from his eyes when she confessed what he already knew. "With you, I'll probably enjoy it a whole lot more."

"I can't go all night without a taste of you at least." Henry pinched the bridge of his nose for a moment. "Don't laugh, but I'd kind of like our first time to be special."

"Isn't that supposed to be my line?" Brooklyn couldn't believe it possible that Henry Emerson had a shy bone in his body. Maybe it was simply inexperience. Debonair he had down pat. Romantic, however, could be as new for him as it was for her.

"If I did anything the traditional way." He cupped her shoulders in his big hands and made sure she was paying close attention. "That isn't my style. You're what I prefer."

"So what's the holdup?" Brooklyn squirmed on his lap enough to torture them both. "I saw that bed back there. It might not be the biggest I've ever done it in, but it certainly looked lush. Lots of pillows. I like that."

"Is that some kind of euphemism?" Henry narrowed his eyes.

"Nope." Brooklyn trailed her fingers down his sculpted chest, then his abs. "I haven't gotten a good enough feel to make any of those kinds of comparisons. Yet. Hiding something?"

She could tell enough to know he didn't have to. Besides, tales from his past lovers were legendary around Underground.

"Screw that." He might have protested more vehemently except they began to taxi just then, so he buckled them in instead of defending his manhood.

They accelerated down the runway and launched into the air, leaving her insides jellied, or maybe Henry had something to do with that. As soon as they got the signal from the captain that they could move about the cabin, Henry stood in a rush, scooping Brooklyn into his arms as if she weighed nothing. Sure, she worked out plenty, but she'd always been the tallest of all her friends. Good thing Henry towered above most men or she'd be doomed to sacrifice her fetish for high heels.

"I'd rather fuck you." Why bother pulling her punches at this point?

"An appetizer for now." Henry toted her to the bedroom and kicked the door shut. He maneuvered through the tight spaces with the grace of a jungle cat, never once so much as banging her elbow.

"I've never been a fan of diets." Brooklyn did her best not to pout.

"I'll make it worth your wait." He silenced her with a kiss that scattered all her objections. All she could focus on was the heat of their lips dancing as he set her on the bed.

Henry didn't break their contact for a moment as he shucked his suit jacket then toed off his expensive shoes, which were polished so thoroughly they'd gleamed even in the partial shade and failing sun of his garden.

Speeding the process along, she unknotted his tie, hoping he'd find better uses for the silk later. Soon he was standing in front of her in only his probably one-of-a-kind Jaeger-LeCoultre watch. She recognized the logo from her father's pride and joy, a relic she had found it impossible to part with.

Propped on her elbows in a mountain of down, she stared at Henry's finely chiseled muscles. He could have been a statue in one of Paris's world-famous museums.

An instant classic, she thought.

Brooklyn's gaze scanned him from his slightly furred chest to his washboard abs. She licked her lips as she studied his long, thick erection, which hardened by the second. His legs enthralled her with their length, strength, and the fine curve of his calves. Still, she came back to his groin. The bulkiness developing there as she appraised him required her to cup her breast to ease some of the heaviness that settled in her chest.

"Thanks." His smug pose, arms crossed, feet spread, only enhanced his sex appeal.

Brooklyn reached behind her for a pillow to launch in his direction.

He fended it off easily then pounced, rolling her to her stomach and straddling her before she could protest. Not that she would have.

Henry unzipped her uniform in record time. Hell, it usually took her a few contortions and shimmies to work her way free of the latex. A master of seduction, he peeled it off, kissed her between her shoulder blades then flipped her over before she'd even finished being grateful for freedom from the restricting garb.

The thick shaft of his cock weighed heavy on her belly when he hovered over her, placing a kiss on the tip of each of her breasts before wandering up to reclaim her mouth. Though she wished their increasingly frantic parries of tongue and lips could satisfy her completely, she needed more.

Henry chose right then to rip his mouth away. He shot her a steamy stare before sinking lower, spreading her legs around his torso as he nibbled a path toward her core. Without wasting a moment, he scented the air as if getting high on her arousal, then dove into the moist flesh between her legs.

If the skill of his tongue hadn't been obvious when he'd kissed the shit out of her, there was no denying his talents when he employed them to flick his deft muscle against her clit, circling, tapping, and fluttering in an assault of pleasure guaranteed to curl her toes in record time.

Before she could warn him, she felt herself spiraling out of control, something that never happened at Underground. Sex was sex. Pleasurable, sure. An epic release of tension and worry. Freedom from her daily life. Not this terrifying flight toward the unknown.

Brooklyn heard herself whimper.

"It's okay." Henry lifted his head long enough to reassure her. "I've got you. Let me see how beautiful you are when you come. For me."

Had he watched her climax for others? Probably, as not all areas of Underground guaranteed privacy.

Henry embedded two fingers in her clenching pussy. Whatever nerves he pressed, they were definitely the right ones to light up her entire body like an old-fashioned switchboard when gossip flew across town.

Brooklyn unraveled in his hands. She stared into his warm, dilated eyes as she surrendered to his wishes, which matched hers exactly. Orgasm washed over her, drowning her in relief that was chased by renewed desire when he pumped his hand between her legs, drawing out the ecstasy.

Only this time, she wanted to taste him, too.

When she reached for his hip, he caught on quickly, rotating without abandoning her pussy until he spanned her again, this time with his knees on either side of her head. She didn't have to strain her neck reaching for his cock. The tip prodded her lips, glossing them with his pre-come.

Brooklyn sucked him into her mouth, savoring the flavor of man and heat. She relished the groan he surrendered and the thrill of the resulting vibration on her pussy. Once more, he dedicated himself to lifting her higher up the corkscrew of rapture she hadn't quite slid all the way down after her dizzying climax.

Brooklyn wondered how long they could torture each other like this.

Not more than a few minutes at first. It seemed Henry was every bit as eager as she was for relief. Maybe then they could focus on getting to know each other, when there was room for rational thought in between her instincts, which screamed at her to bend over for the man dominating her so naturally.

She employed every fancy move she'd mastered in the past few years to lave his cock so well he'd never forget her or this night. At least she hoped he wouldn't be able to.

Still he managed to get her off a handful of times before she felt him tensing above her.

Brooklyn grabbed Henry's ass and dug her fingernails into the knotted muscles there, dragging him forward until she'd captured every inch of his impressive shaft, even though it meant he was buried in her throat. And when she swallowed around him, she had the satisfaction of hearing his primal growl and a half-hearted warning.

A few pulls of her mouth later and he was pouring his release into her. She showed her appreciation for the dazzling pleasure he'd gifted her with by joining him, satisfied she'd made her point when he kissed her inner thighs between whispered curses and praise.

Henry softened. He withdrew despite her gentled suckling then gathered her to his chest where he wrapped them both in fine linens and her in his arms.

"Sleep, Brooklyn." He nuzzled the crown of her head with his chin. "It'll be morning when we arrive. And there's so much I want to show you."

Though she attempted to stifle her yawn and vote for more bedroom games, Brooklyn found herself obeying his gravelly commands. Her eyes drifted shut and she burrowed into the warmth and security of his hold.

Doing something she hadn't ever before, she fell asleep in a man's embrace, looking forward to waking in exactly the same place.

Hell, they never even had to get off the plane. This had already been the trip of a lifetime.

Brooklyn wasn't usually the hand-holding type. Oddly, she found herself glad Henry refused to release her when she shook their connected fingers as they prepared to descend the jet's staircase.

Dressed in a gorgeous watercolor silk cover-up, which draped artfully over one of the skimpy bikinis he'd supplied—along with more clothes than she probably had in her closet at home—she felt like a fairy tale had swooped in and replaced her life.

If only Henry had caved to her pawing this morning, she could die happy.

Instead, he'd shown her how well he could use a showerhead to pleasure her again—and, *oops*, again—before buckling her in for their landing. She'd been too weak to protest their lopsided affair.

With one hand she held the rail, dizzied by the steps she took downward. Partially because she scanned the horizon for any break in the cerulean waves. There was none to be found. And partially because of Henry's effect on her. He still clenched her fingers in his, despite the awkward twist of his arm behind his back.

The wide brim of her floppy hat didn't obscure the beauty around them. Even through the polarized sunglasses perched on her nose, she could detect the vibrant emerald of the palm treetops against the backdrop of a cloudless azure

sky with golden sand at their feet. The dunes reminded her of
Scrooge McDuck's piles of coins. She wondered if Henry
swam through his wealth when no one watched. After the
past twenty-four hours, she no longer doubted that if he piled
his riches next to the cartoon mogul's, he'd come out ahead.

They stood side by side, admiring the landscape, which
could have come straight from the calendar, *Spectacular
Hideaways*, that hung in her kitchen.

"So, what now?" Brooklyn hoped it had a lot to do with
shedding their clothes and rolling around in one of the
oversized hammocks she spotted hanging in the shade
between two curved trunks near the beach.

"We relax. I'm getting the feeling that might be as
difficult for you as it is for me." Henry kicked off his flip-
flops, shed his open white cotton shirt on the boardwalk
leading from the crude airport, and snaked his arm around
her waist. "Ever been snorkeling?"

"It was part of my SCUBA training last summer, but
only in the facility's pool." She frowned. Torn, she would
love to explore the underwater realm that encircled the
island. The reef had been visible from above in the varied
hues of aqua that dotted the isolated land mass. Out here, she
bet the pristine environment held an abundance of colorful
life. Then again...she'd had other relaxation methods on the
brain.

What was it about Henry that compelled her?

"The Aquatic Adventure shop off Hamilton Ave?"
Henry's inquiry came a little too nonchalant. "How'd you
like your instructor?"

"Don't tell me..." Her radar flashed red alert. "You're
one of their investors?"

"Sort of." He shrugged.

Brooklyn stopped short. The resulting jerk on Henry's
arm drew him up too. "Don't play games with me. I've been
completely honest with you, no matter how embarrassing. I

don't throw myself at many men, you know."

"You're cute when you're pissed." He smirked before shutting her down with a soft kiss. "I'm sorry. I'm used to hiding who I really am. And this means something to me, okay? I'm not eager to ruin what we have over shit as insignificant as money."

"Wealth isn't an issue. Subterfuge is." Brooklyn refused to back down despite the melting of her insides, which had nothing to do with the sunny day.

"I own the dive shop. It's not a big deal, okay? It's a lucrative industry if you have the capital to get the facilities up and running. Besides, it's something I enjoy."

Jeez. How much of the city did he control?

Brooklyn swallowed hard and pretended it didn't matter. "My instructor, David, was terrific. He explained everything really well and made me feel at ease, even the first time I breathed underwater."

"It is odd, isn't it?" Henry stared at her. "Like you might drown. But you don't. It goes against every instinct and yet feels so natural once you're doing it."

"Yeah. That's it exactly." She thought it might be kind of like submerging herself in Henry's world and this insane chemistry they had together.

They strolled quietly toward a small building on the beach, neither of them feeling the need to say more than they just had. And when they reached the structure, Henry let himself inside the unlocked door. She supposed there was no need for security on a private island after all.

"Come on," Henry urged as he handed her a mask and fins. "Let's get your feet wet. In the meantime, I'll have David e-mail your records over so we know what equipment you're used to and how much weight you need in the integrated pockets of your BC vest."

Suddenly, she didn't feel like arguing. Forty-eight hours of this couldn't be enough to sustain her forever after, but she planned to make as many memories as possible to hang on to once they returned to real life.

Every minute they frolicked in paradise together built anticipation. Brooklyn enjoyed Henry's tour of the coast and the fish they saw when they snorkeled above the reef offshore. She'd be lying if she said she hadn't forgotten about the agenda for their weekend away for a little while when Henry guided her through the submarine landscape in her first official dive since gaining her open water certification in a local quarry, which she thought hardly counted after experiencing the ocean.

Jewel-toned fish darted all around them. Soft corals swayed in the swell, the deep red fans fluttering near the squiggly yellow clump of brain coral that caught her attention next. Her mask had fogged when the sight of a seahorse clinging to a sponge took her breath away and brought tears to her eyes. Rare and precious, the gift Henry gave her grew more and more exquisite with each natural wonder they discovered together.

Holding hands, they bobbed in the shallows on their safety stop. Three minutes seemed like an eternity yet passed as quickly as a flash of lightning while they stared into each other's eyes. Without the ability to speak, they communicated on a whole new level she'd never experienced before.

Warm water and the current of their connection kept her comfortable until they could ascend and swim back to shore. Together.

Though Brooklyn hadn't seen another soul since they'd touched down, a fantastic picnic lunch awaited them inside a canvas-topped shelter. Square, with panels of gauzy material tied on the sides, it allowed the breeze to pass through while providing shade for the blanket and baskets. As the tide came in, the lapping waves kept barely out of reach of their sanctuary.

With their gear replaced in the shed, they devoured the selection of coconut shrimp, grilled fish—which tasted better than anything she'd ever had "fresh" back home—and a selection of tropical fruits. When Henry leaned over to feed her a slice of pineapple, she couldn't help but lick the sweet juice from his fingers.

And next thing she knew, he'd pushed her onto her back on a soft blanket and covered her with his glistening, tan body.

Welcome relief emanated from the places he pressed against her while he kissed her as if she were the sweetest kind of dessert imaginable. Their fingers entwined and he raised her hands, pinning them to the sand above the fringe of their coverlet.

The only part of her unsatisfied after a wonderful day— the sexual side of her she kept as hidden as Henry's wealth— stretched and purred.

"Take me," she whispered. "Please."

Instead of gaining momentum, Henry paused. He lifted up enough to survey her needy expression. The ridge of his erection prodded her belly. At least she wasn't the only one dying here.

"Why are you waiting?" She tried not to sulk.

"I guess I'm trying to make today perfect. I know what you're like in the club, but what about in a relationship? Are you a 'behind closed doors' kind of girl? Or a 'let the world watch' woman?" Henry tilted his head as he appraised her.

"I have a feeling I'm something entirely new with you." Number one indicator being that she wanted to pounce on him rather than run screaming when he said the usually dreaded *relationship* word.

Never before had she been excited about the loss of her freedom.

"Same goes, Brooklyn." Henry's brow furrowed. "In fact, I think you should know I've *never* had something more meaningful than a fling before. I don't plan to screw this up."

Did that mean that what they shared went beyond that to him? She didn't intend to get her hopes up yet.

Nothing would ruin this moment. This weekend.

"So tell me, which would you prefer...?" Henry asked her between nibbling kisses on her jaw and neck, as if he couldn't stand to stop for even a minute or two. "Do you want to check out the bungalow over there or are you good with being ravished on the beach? Choose quickly, I have to be inside you. Soon."

If Brooklyn said *I'd like a tour of your house*, turn to page 172, *Overwater Cabana (4H)*.

If Brooklyn said *I'm good right here*, turn to page 160, *Sex on the Beach (4G)*.

Spank Me, Henry (4A)

"The only thing naughty about you is the way you stayed away from me all this time," Henry teased as he drew her through the door she'd indicated. "We could have done this years ago."

"Me?" Brooklyn lifted her brows at him.

"Okay, fine, I didn't make a move either. But isn't it bad form for the boss to solicit his employees?" He drew her to him again and kissed her softly. "I did hit on you the instant you quit, remember?"

Actually, she tried not to because that meant she'd traded a place that had become her home base for one night of pleasure. A super fine night, sure. Still…she didn't intend to tarnish the evening with preemptive regret.

"Let's not argue. If you need a reason to spank me, that'll do." Brooklyn smiled a little shyly. She'd never asked this of a man before, couldn't say really why the need had bubbled up in her with Henry around.

Some part of her had never forgiven herself for choosing to stay home the night of her family's accident. She hadn't felt well, but still, she could have muddled through one of her father's charity events.

Though she knew she'd been spared, part of her still suffered under a horrendous burden of shame. Maybe he could help her exorcise those demons. Strip her down and help her release the agony, replace it with something far more pleasurable.

"Sweetheart, what are you thinking about?" Henry grew quiet as he studied her. Obviously she didn't have nearly as good a poker face as he did.

"My family." Within these walls, there was no room for lies. She broke their gaze rather than witness the pity in his warm eyes. Instead, she took in the velvety surfaces and gold embossed wallpaper that dressed up the space. One entire side of the chamber had been devoted to spanking implements—paddles, crops, gloves with metal brads—in all materials from wood to rubber.

"Brooklyn, look at me." She swallowed hard and tried to stifle the distraction by concentrating on his concern. "You don't really hope I'll hurt you because you're battling some kind of survivor's guilt, do you? I'm sorry. I won't do that. Let's go next door instead."

"No. Not exactly," she amended.

"Then why are these ghosts haunting your pretty eyes?" He caressed her shoulders then her arms, finally holding her hands safe in his.

"It's not that I want you to punish me for living when they died." Forcing herself to continue despite the tightness in her throat was difficult. "But when it happened, I locked away the sadness. I had to compartmentalize my brain in order to survive. And I think I might have gotten too good at it."

"You can't live fully if you haven't let yourself mourn." He understood so easily. "I'll help you unlock your primitive side, Brooklyn. I'll take you to a place where all that exists is pure emotion. I'll do anything you ask to help. But are you sure you're ready?"

She took a second to really consider what he offered.

Tears prickled her eyes before she could blink them away. That he would pass up a superficial hookup in favor of a whole tangle of messy baggage only enhanced her already high opinion of her date. He could have any woman he wanted outside this room and not have to worry about all this extra shit.

Instead, he stuck with her.

No way in hell would she turn him down.

"Yes, but…" Did she dare make another request? Hadn't she asked enough of him already?

"Go ahead." He rubbed his thumbs over her knuckles.

"Can it be with your bare hand? I need to feel connected, not distanced by some inanimate object." The faint zing of copper made her aware she'd bit her lip. "I mean, if that's okay with you..."

"I wouldn't have it any other way. Henry shifted his hands to her waist and lifted her as if she weren't tall and proportionally heavy. Next thing she knew, the world spun around her as he sat in a super-sized ornate chair which had somehow lost its arms. The piece made it easy for him to sit and drape her, face down, across his lap.

Without much introduction, he rubbed his palm over her exposed bottom in circles that soothed even as they made her suspicious of when the first smack would come. Her hair waterfalled to the floor where her hands braced for extra stability.

Henry's necklace fell forward so that she practically kissed the electric-blue stone. She liked the reminder of him there, especially when the gentle pressure of his palm disappeared followed shortly by the swish of wind then a stinging spank.

Preparing for a shock that burst on her ass then fizzled through her whole body, changing from pain to something far more fun as it went, would have been impossible anyway. He didn't stop with a single impact. Again and again, he landed sharp cracks that made her sure this wasn't his inaugural run with paddling someone's behind.

For the first dozen or so whacks, her thoughts bounced around from *son of a bitch that hurts* to *ohhh, it feels kind of tingly and warm too* to *I hate every woman he's spanked besides me*. But after that, something began to change. Instead of racing, her mind quieted, focused only on her breathing, which made the pain bearable as sensation layered on already stimulated nerves.

A while longer and her squirming, which was easily squashed by his arm across her back, even stopped. Bright white sparks flew behind her eyes, allowing her to zone out and separate herself from all the troubling worries of day-to-day life.

Brooklyn had seen submissives at the club with that happy, far-off look in their eyes. Right then she knew she'd read the same on her face if she had a mirror. Accepting her fate, she settled into the calm that stemmed from acceptance.

Henry's spanks came quicker now, multiplying the effect of her endorphin rush as well as the cathartic discomfort that frothed up inside her, granting her permission to express the pain with cries and whimpers she'd suffocated in the long empty nights she'd spent alone.

As if he could sense she'd hit her wall, or maybe broken through it, Henry changed his approach. Instead of a flurry of consistent smacks, he escalated the spanks he delivered, but spaced them out. Through her trance, she heard him counting down.

Three…two…

At the last hard smack, which zinged her already electrified nerve endings, Brooklyn flew beyond her corporeal bounds. Pain unlocked her instincts. She cowered, not in fear of him, but of herself. Would she fly apart if he didn't ground her soon?

Henry had already begun to rub her ass, soothing the throbbing red cheeks, replacing his spanking with a tender comforting she knew would destroy her.

Scorched by the fire of her burning skin, she allowed herself to emit a tiny mewl. The problem was that once she cracked, she couldn't stop chunks of her psyche from joining the party. One dainty sniffle escalated into a sob, and soon she found herself bawling.

As soon as the dam broke, Henry hauled her up and hugged her to his chest.

Whatever nonsense he murmured to her was lost beneath her crying, but the soothing sound cut through anyway.

Though she should have been embarrassed by her reaction, especially in the arms of a new lover, she relied on her instincts, which promised he wouldn't mind. That he'd relish the opportunity to give back to her.

True to her imaginings, he lifted her into his arms and toted her to the lush bed. He tucked her beneath the covers as she sobbed. Quickly, he stripped off his leather pants and joined her. The entire time she vented, the incessant caress of his hands over her back, ass, upper thighs, shoulders, and neck confirmed her place in the universe and that she was in fact still here to feel the pain of loss as well as the bliss of great sex.

Maybe that's why she'd turned to Underground.

It made her feel alive—connected to something positive.

Her blubbering faded to the occasional hiccup over time. Perhaps losing her job wasn't the crisis she'd assumed. After tonight, she might not need that crutch anymore.

All thanks to Henry.

He held out a silk handkerchief to her with *HE* embroidered on the corner in royal-blue thread.

"I don't want to get it dirty. It's too pretty."

"Then it's fitting." He tucked her hair behind her ear and kissed her forehead before insisting again. "You're gorgeous even when you're breaking my heart. Feel better, sweetheart?"

"For now." She didn't believe their session would be a magic Band-Aid over her cracked soul, but she did think— like lancing a blister—that it had relieved a lot of the pressure that had built up there over the past two years. "Thank you."

Henry rocked her against his chest some more.

"I'm sorry if that was kind of a buzz kill." She let her forehead crash onto his shoulder.

"Uh," he hesitated, drawing her attention with his rare uncertainty. "Don't take this the wrong way, okay?"

She shrugged.

When he realigned their bodies so that she was completely blanketed by him, it was apparent why. The thick length of his shaft tipped onto her belly, impressing her all over again with the heft of his long cock.

"Seriously?" She peered up at him with bugged eyes.

"It turns me on that you'd let me see this side of you." He peppered her face with butterfly kisses. "I'm so used to the badass bombshell who rules Underground without ever having to say a word. To witness your vulnerability. And know you wouldn't show it to another person here tonight…"

Brooklyn sighed, relieved that he understood her so well.

"Well, that means something to me. And it turns me on." He kissed her then, a consuming lip lock that went on long enough to blank her mind and jumpstart wanton urges.

Her legs spread wider, allowing his trim hips to fit snuggly between them.

When he sank into the space that seemed made for him, his cock poked and prodded her opening. They both flexed, introducing the tip of him to her pussy.

"Condom." He grimaced as if he'd only now remembered.

Before he could leave her to rummage for one, she banded her arms and legs around him.

"I'm clean. You know I am." She thought of her routine exams, required by the club. As if he might have forgotten his own rules, she reminded him. "And all hosts are on birth control, too."

"Yeah, but you don't know the same about me." He grimaced. "Not the birth control part, obviously, but the safe part. I swear I am."

She laughed. The lightness in her heart floored her.

Henry had broken her free by melting the ice of a long winter. How could he doubt her trust after all they'd shared?

"I believe you." She kissed him gently, though that

didn't last long. Soon they were feasting on each other, writhing until their bodies aligned naturally once more.

This time when his cock began to penetrate, he didn't pull away.

For added insurance, Brooklyn canted her hips up, swallowing more of him with her saturated pussy. Having him inside her, even the barest bit, shone a light on so many dark places, chasing shadows away.

She welcomed him, helping him knit their bodies completely bit by bit.

And when he bottomed out, stretching her pussy with both his length and girth, they sighed in unison. Still for one moment, they perched on the cusp of something amazing and stared down into the swirling vortex of rapture together.

Then they tipped over.

Henry began to fuck her with long liquid glides between her legs. The soreness of her ass only enhanced his motion. The reminder of her release spurred her toward another kind of relief. Both supplied by the damn-near perfect guy delivering thrust after thrust in perfect sync with her hips, which raised to meet him each time he fed his cock into her body.

He withdrew to the brink of falling free then plunged into her, balls deep.

The leather of his harness rubbed her diamond-tipped breasts in a delicious addition to the sensations they generated together. But it was the look in his eyes when he descended to kiss her—slow and sweet, then fast and hard— that rocked her world.

Her pussy clamped on his pistoning cock.

"That's right," he whispered against her lips. "Hold on to me. Tight."

As if she'd let go. Not when he raised her this high. But the increasing grip of her pussy multiplied his pleasure as he worked harder to infiltrate the rings of her muscles and repaid her in kind as the blunt cap of his dick massaged her from the inside out.

When he shortened his stride, jabbing her repeatedly in exactly the right spot, she knew their time in heaven was limited.

"I'm right there with you, sweetheart," he rumbled. "Come. With me."

When Brooklyn obeyed, it seemed as if the whole world paused. All she saw was Henry's intent stare as her entire body braced for implosion. He groaned her name as he pumped his release inside her over and over.

She saw his lips move, but didn't actually hear it because she screamed louder than the time a spider at least as big as a European car had pranced across her keyboard while she was in the middle of Googling something.

"I'll take that as a compliment." He chuckled, though the strain of his dying climax tinged his mirth.

"You'd better." Brooklyn didn't fight when he tucked her against his chest and wrapped her in his strong arms. "I'm pretty sure all of Underground heard that. Your reputation just went up. You'll be beating women off with a stick soon. As if you weren't already."

"Is that jealousy, sweetheart?" He traced the brilliant blue opal he'd given her earlier where it dangled between her breasts. "That shade of green looks great on you."

She didn't respond, choosing to rest her head over his still pounding heart instead. For tonight, she belonged to him, and vice versa.

"We'll talk about this more in the morning, okay?" He dragged his knuckles lightly across her bare back in a repetitive motion that hypnotized her. Or maybe it was the matched set of emotional and physical releases he'd granted her that did that.

"Sure," she mumbled before slipping into a nightmare-free sleep for the first time she could remember.

For the epilogue turn to page *182, Epilogue: Henry's Surprise (5A)*.

Sex Swing (4B)

"Good choice." Henry grinned at her as he hauled her into the sex swing room. "I can't wait to see you fly."

Whether he referred to her in the prurient contraption or her coming, she didn't know for sure. Probably both.

Either got a big *hell yeah* from her, too.

Automatically triggered lights cast a soft glow around the interior of the room, which grew a bit more shadowy when Henry kicked the door closed behind them, locking them inside.

An ordinary—if lavish—arena, maroon wallpaper dotted with gold fleur-de-lis was accented by a plush navy carpet with a fret border. The almost stately space featured a canopied bed in complementary walnut. Masculine and almost imperial, it could have been a room in a grand hotel, until she followed Henry's gaze to the opposite end of the quarters.

There, not one sex swing but a whole host of options were lined up like she might want to take each for a test drive before deciding on the perfect ride for her. She giggled to herself at her ridiculous mental image of Henry as a diabolical pleasure salesman who helped her make the ultimate selection.

"Something funny?" He came up behind her, looping his arms around her waist as though they'd been partners for years instead of an hour.

"More that I can't believe this is where the day has brought me." She angled her face to the side so she could catch his answering smile. "It's not at all how I imagined today would go."

He swooped in for a drugging kiss, causing her lids to half shutter and all thoughts to flee. Except for those about how serious the solid erection nudging the small of her back seemed to be.

"I hope that's a good thing," he murmured when he finally released her.

"Definitely." She smiled as he spun her around to face him.

"Then I just have one request." Henry grinned at her, reflecting her elation and even some of the peace she experienced in his company. She hadn't realized how tightly strung he was most of the time, until she saw him like this. Relaxed. Intimate.

"What's that?" She'd give him pretty much anything. Already had by trying something new that required so much trust with him. Hell, she'd even sacrificed the best—okay, only—job she'd ever had for him.

"Help me peel these damn pants off." He flicked open the button at the top then drew the zipper carefully over the bulge in the crotch of the leather, which looked stretched to the ripping point.

Brooklyn laughed. She hadn't expected a liaison with Henry to be so damn easy. Organic. With him, everything seemed simple—attraction, affection, a good time. Nothing to complain about there. She'd been a host long enough to know some awkwardness crept into every first encounter. Most nights, it was her job to jump that hurdle and grant both her and her partner a positive experience.

Here, she didn't have to work at all. And not because she was off the clock.

When she put her hands on his trim hips and slid her fingers beneath the taut material highlighting his high, tight ass to perfection, he let his head drop back. A groan left his mouth when she shimmied the material down his powerful thighs then helped him step out of the pants with first one foot, then the other.

The relief should have been substantial, as his erection continued to expand once the restriction had been removed. His fingers unfisted and his jaw relaxed.

Of course, when faced with his solid cock, she couldn't help but play a little.

Brooklyn wrapped her hand around his shaft and lifted it until the fat, blunt head pointed at the ceiling. She leaned in and nuzzled his balls, loving the moan he let loose when she moved on to kissing them then licking his Vesling's line along the center of his scrotum.

She figured he did pretty well to resist making another peep or grabbing her head until she sucked his testicles one by one into her mouth. Most guys wouldn't have lasted that long without trying to direct her. And the spearing of his fingers into her hair seemed more like holding on to keep from busting his ass than commanding her.

Either way, she didn't mind. In fact, the slight tug on her scalp turned her on. It encouraged her to take more of him and to begin pumping her hand up and down his impressive length while she played with his balls.

She lapped him from his taint, over his sac, then from the base of his cock to its tip, adoring the quiver of his tree-trunk thighs when she circled the ridge that delineated the head of his dick from the substantial, veiny shaft. A teensy flick over his frenulum and he broke his silence.

"Suck me, Brooklyn." Though he didn't add a please to the end of his request, she knew he was begging all the same. A man like Henry Emerson didn't have to ask for much in life.

So she granted his wish.

She opened her mouth and welcomed him inside, laving the underside of him with the flat of her tongue while her fingers continued to roll his testicles between them. Long before her jaw suffered even a hint of soreness, he cupped his hands beneath her elbows and hauled her to her feet.

Despite the tang of his pre-come on her tongue, he didn't hesitate a single second before kissing the shit out of her. "Some other time, I'll let you finish that. Though I'd like to deck the men that taught you how to blow me so well, I suppose it's rude to punch a gift horse in the mouth, huh?"

His gruff dirty talk had her thighs slickening as he walked her backward, advancing with a gleam in his eye that told her she'd pushed him about as far as was wise.

Except that she loved spurring him beyond his usual ironclad control.

The implication that tonight might not be a one-time show wasn't half bad either. It did funny things to the pit of her stomach, as well as somewhere a little higher up in her chest.

When something tapped above her ass, she froze. Stuck between one of the harnesses and Henry's advance, she reveled in the thrill caused by his impending assumption of control. Over her. Over them and their shared encounter.

"Is that the one you want to try?" He jerked his chin in the direction of the swing, which now tapped her, having begun to move after her contact. "It's the one I would have recommended for a beginner at this, though a woman who's well versed in other sexual pursuits."

She rotated so she could get a better look at what her future held. "Why this one?"

"Some of them are too cushy. Like the ones on the end." He pointed. "See how they have full lounging platforms and even pillows. Hell, that one is essentially a mini bed on chains. While that might be fun, it's not as exhilarating as one that will really make you feel like you're flying."

"So why not go more extreme?" She could tell as she looked down the line that the options to her opposite side had less material and relied more on hoops of leather to elevate various body parts. The most intense would essentially turn her into a marionette with a chain attached to each joint and not much in between.

"To me, that's edging into pure suspension. It might not be much of a distinction, but that's not what I'd assume you had in mind for tonight." He rubbed his cock as if he couldn't stand the thought without touching himself. "I'm game if you are, but..."

"You're right." She nodded. "This one seems about right."

"Then up you go, Goldilocks." He grinned and kissed her as he wrapped his hands around her waist. He manhandled her as if she were petite and model thin instead of the tall woman she'd blossomed into.

Before she could think to be frightened, he'd arranged her so that her ass and back were supported by a wide strip of leather and got to work on cuffing her extremities to the chains with the attached manacles. Though the fur-lined rings were inescapable, she found them comfortable and oddly comforting, too.

Security washed over her, both because of the solid grip of the device and because of the man wielding his sexual power over her. Neither would let her fall.

Fully committed to the leather swing, she settled into her bonds and the gear supporting her. Sure, she was wide open and ready for whatever Henry decided to do to her, but that didn't matter so much as lifting the burden of decision-making from her shoulders.

Ever since she'd found herself utterly alone in the world, she'd had to bear all the responsibility. Handing some of it off to him... Amazing.

"Is it what you'd hoped for?" Henry seemed genuinely concerned.

"There's a freedom in this." She closed her eyes and allowed him to rock her as if she were a baby in a cradle. "I don't have to think. Don't have to fend for myself. Sorry, but you get to do all the work."

Brooklyn peeked up at Henry, who smiled broadly in return.

"This is the kind of labor I'm not afraid of." He dipped a

finger between her legs, into the soaking folds of her pussy. The motion he'd established kept her arc going and fucked her onto his digit then off—on and off.

While it was a delicious treat, she needed the whole meal.

"Henry," she whimpered.

"Yes, sweetheart?" He forced her to admit it aloud.

"I need you to fuck me. Please." She stared at his generous cock, which had responded to freedom by growing even harder. The thickness was at least as impressive as his length. Fully erect, his dick hung between his thighs, heavy and dripping.

"Let me grab a condom." He would have turned, but she reacted violently, causing her chains to jangle.

"No, don't." She couldn't say why it mattered so much, but suddenly she had to have him with nothing between them. "Take me bare. I'm clean. You know I am. We're tested regularly here, and I'm on birth control, too, as my contract required."

"Of course." He frowned at her. "I was more concerned that you can't say the same for me."

"You're safe, right?" She bit her lip while she waited for him to affirm.

"Yeah. I just didn't expect you to believe me without papers." He swallowed hard. "Are you serious?"

"Yes. And if I didn't trust you, I wouldn't have let you truss me up like this." Another clink followed when she rattled her chains.

"Okay, good point." His lips tipped up at the corners. "In that case..."

He grabbed her leg with one hand and his hard-on with the other. He shuffled forward until he had aligned their bodies, then drew her to him, piercing her with his cock.

It was a good thing she was shackled or she would have jerked right off his shaft and onto the floor. Not very sexy.

But the pressure of him entering her felt divine. He stretched her as he advanced down her channel, widening her with every inch he fed into her pussy.

Just when she expected him to begin to shuttle, holding her steady as he pounded inside her, he made the beauty of the swing apparent.

It was a novel way to be fucked. Instead of Henry powering into her, he grabbed the chains of the swing and yanked *her* toward *him*. A minimal flex of his hips did all the rest. Inertia and the occasional tug by the man impaling her kept their rhythm going.

"You know, I could fuck you like this all night." No surprise, he echoed her thoughts.

Except she knew neither one of them could resist coming when he filled her to perfection time and time again. They might have to have a do-over later tonight because this ride wasn't going to last very long for either of them.

He allowed her arc to become shallower so that only the very tip of him slipped in and out of her opening. The ridge beneath his head felt divine as it teased the rings of muscle right there on the cusp of her body. He allowed himself to pull fully out of her before penetrating her again.

Her eyes rolled back as he nudged a particularly responsive section of her pussy. "Henry!"

"Right there, huh?" He toyed with her, intentionally skipping the magic zone to plunge deeper and harder than before. "Want me to do that again?"

"Yes!" She would have strangled him if she could have.

"A bunch?" The intensity of his laser-beam stare assured he'd enjoyed it as much as her. So why was he torturing them both?

"Damn you, Henry Emerson." She spit the curse at him. "I'll beg for you. Please. Please give me your cock in that perfect spot. Again and again. Until I come all over you."

"Christ." He snarled. "I love a woman who talks dirty."

So she kept it up while he rewarded her by giving her exactly what she'd asked for. He swung her so that his cock rubbed that bliss-inducing place inside her again and again with unerring accuracy.

Her toes curled where they were elevated above his shoulders. He smiled wolfishly before kissing the edge of her foot. "That's it, Brooklyn. I want to watch you come apart, feel you wringing my cock dry."

"Only if you're with me." She didn't give a shit that she panted. "Pour your release into me, Henry. Give it to me. All of it."

She couldn't say which of them caved first, only that as she began to spasm, he painted her with the proof of his enjoyment. Splashes of come washed over her enflamed tissue as he pumped himself inside her and she orgasmed around him.

The swing had one benefit she hadn't considered. It gave her a front row seat to the Henry Emerson show. His entire frame corded, muscles flexed and glistening with perspiration. The intensity in his eyes, which never once glanced away from her while they shared this epic explosion of passion, blew her away.

She swore she came for hours.

Brooklyn floated, soaking in the fantastic relief that pounded through her. She hardly registered Henry unbuckling her restraints or lifting her from the swing. Instead of getting curious, she decided to go the lazy route and curled against his chest instead. With her arms looped around his neck and his strength supporting her, she couldn't have cared less where he took her.

Turned out, he ventured only as far as the bed in the corner of the room. The black satin sheets caressed her over-sensitized skin as he slipped her between them then climbed in after her. They cuddled together, even their legs wrapping around each other and their bare feet rubbing wherever and however they could reach.

Henry kissed the side of her face and worked his way to nuzzling her hair. Then he whispered in her ear, "I can feel the necklace between us. I like that you're still wearing it."

She knew she'd never take the damn thing off. Not if it reminded her of this moment.

"I wish I had something to give you." Brooklyn frowned.

It didn't last long though when he turned her mouth up again with a lingering kiss. Then he said, "You already gave me everything I could have asked for. Thank you. Tonight was…"

"Brilliant." She finished for him.

Though she tried to keep her eyes open to stare at the man of her dreams, gravity tugged on her lids. Sated sleepiness shooed her toward unconsciousness.

"Goodnight, sweetheart." Henry held her tighter as they floated together.

And she knew he had it right. Any night with him would be spectacular.

For the epilogue turn to page *182, Epilogue: Henry's Surprise*.

Water Bondage (4C)

"I always wanted to be a mermaid," Brooklyn confessed.

"Then I'll have to take you to my private island sometime." Henry gave her some glimmer of future prospects, though maybe it was just something to say to ease their transition to the private room he practically jogged to. "You'd look beautiful snorkeling over the reef or maybe getting fucked on the beach."

She might have had some smarmy comeback for him if he hadn't tipped the latch with his hip then sidled into their destination. Automatic lights came to life, shining through a sheet of aqua Plexiglas that created the illusion of sunlight through water. Or maybe a rainy day with partial sun.

Pipes lined the perimeter of the ceiling. The entire room had been sealed with watertight materials and the sloped floor—covered with Astroturf, or maybe even real grass— kept walking from being treacherous on a wet surface. The lawn led to an engineered stream, landscaped to look real enough to fool her from here. Lush green plants surrounded the collection pool where water was purified and recirculated for a variety of uses. It also allowed for guests to try their hand at underwater sex or a refreshing dip after they'd finished their session.

A constant shower of drips made her glad she didn't have to pee.

Rainbows arched from point to point as light refracted through the constantly changing landscape. Opposite the pond, a low bed with a rubber mattress seemed to be Henry's target. When he laid her on it, she shot her arm out to cling to the frame. It moved beneath her.

A waterbed. Of course.

Brooklyn laughed, delighted by her fantastic surroundings and the man she shared them with. Thank God she'd never caved in to the urge to do more than peek inside here before. She'd made it her goal never to ruin the surprise of one of the club's elaborate settings until she experienced it herself. What Oscar and Henry devised constantly enchanted her.

From overhead, a light shower began, making it seem as if they frolicked in a warm summer rain. Individual droplets coalesced on their bodies and pooled together then trickled around her on the bed.

"I take it you like it?" Henry smiled as moisture beaded on their skin like dew. Soon rivulets trickled across her breasts and her belly, making her eager for more stimulation. She bent her knees so she could splash her toes in a puddle forming in the depression her feet made.

"I love it." She peered around until she spied the dunk tank not even she had evaded hearing about. At the center of the room, the enormous stainless steel and glass vessel was big enough to comfortably fit a basketball team. A nylon harness dangled above the surface of the water within.

"Worry about that later." He blocked her view by settling over her on the waterbed. "We don't have to go there if you're not ready."

"I am." She squirmed beneath him, maximizing the contact of their damp skin. Her hair stuck to her face in wet strands that Henry wrapped around his finger, then tucked out of the way.

"Maybe I'm not." He cleared his throat. "I want to take you gently first. I know you picked the Basement, but…would you mind?"

"I won't complain." Her fingers wandered to his stubbled cheek as she adored the blend of passion and affection he manufactured so easily.

"Good girl." An almost-sweet kiss interrupted their discussion.

Henry lulled her with the placid swipes of his lips, so much so that she didn't notice him fiddling with something at the edge of the bed until it was too late.

A hose wrapped around her wrist, binding it tight.

She gasped, struggling though unable to break his hold.

"You didn't think you were going to escape the bondage part of the room, did you?" He smirked, spinning an extra length of rubber in his hand so it whistled in the air.

She bit her lip and shook her head.

Next thing she knew, he had her ankles wound in the tubing and tied to each corner of the bed. Her thighs spread wide enough to stretch the muscles there to their limits, or slightly beyond, despite her regular yoga regimens—a requirement for her job.

Her hands followed suit. He pinned her wrists together, using the hose around the first to lash them, then raised her arms over her head. The tautness of the next tie, attached somewhere above her, prominently displayed her breasts—a fact that didn't go unnoticed by Henry.

He lowered himself, slipping across her wet body with his own dewy skin. They both groaned at the contact. Despite the warmth of the water, her nipples were rock hard as they skimmed across his chest.

The heavy weight of his erection teased her mound then slipped past her, leaving her near to begging when he wriggled lower. With her chest at mouth level, he took advantage of the offering he'd made of her breasts, sipping water from them one by one.

And when he seemed like he might dip even lower, she tried to close her legs around him, but the restraints stopped her.

"What? You don't like when I eat you?" He grinned, knowing damn well he possessed a rare talent in that arena.

"More like I'll die if you don't fuck me soon. Enough teasing, Henry. I need you." Didn't it say something that the plea didn't even bother her, or at least not more than the pulsing of her empty pussy?

110

"But I've just begun." He mock-pouted. "I haven't even played with these yet."

Her eyes widened when she realized there were more hoses than required for immobilizing someone. Each one he picked up and sprayed into the air had a different flow, some a gush of water, others a trickle. Several pulsed in mesmerizing rhythms.

Having played with her whirlpool tub at home a time or two during long baths, it didn't take her more than a split second—even with a lust-addled brain—to see the possibilities there.

"That's right." Henry aimed two of the laminar streams at her chest, massaging her taut nipples with the water. Then he drew wandering lines all over her body with them. Each time he passed near her mound, he dipped a little farther, teasing her pussy with the resulting splashes.

Even the soles of her feet weren't excluded from his attention.

Then he whipped one of the hoses toward her, targeting her clit with a pulsating current.

That alone nearly tipped her into orgasm after so much stimulation.

Henry's smile bore a resemblance to a grimace. "I'd love to tease you all day, but this is torture for me, too."

"So don't stop. Just fuck me." She gathered her thoughts and spoke between ragged pants.

"I like the way you think, Brooklyn." Henry frowned though as he said it.

"What?" She closed her eyes for a moment, hating anything that could ruin their fun.

"I need to get a condom. I almost forgot." He blasted himself in the face with one of the cooler jets as if to wake himself from the dream they spun together.

"No, don't." She squirmed as much as her bonds allowed, hoping he wouldn't deny her request. "I'm clean.

You know I am from my file and all the testing you do on your hosts and guests. Plus, we're all required to use birth control."

"But you don't know the same about me. I should have showed you my file when we were upstairs." He sighed.

"I trust you, Henry." As if her situation, completely at his mercy, didn't already prove it.

"Seriously?" He swallowed hard enough to flex his powerful throat.

Brooklyn nodded.

With a growl, he skidded between her thighs, using the slippery material of their bed to his best advantage. He scooped her ass into his big hands, letting the tubes now trapped between them spray along her stomach. Then his cock was there, prodding her opening.

With friction minimized both by the environment and the arousal seeping from her, he grazed her folds and nudged her clit on the first several attempts at penetration. Brooklyn moaned and arched.

The curve of her body put her at exactly the right angle to mesh with Henry.

He pressed inside her the barest bit, her body hugging the tip of his cock in welcome.

"Yes." He hissed as he advanced, sliding down her slick channel.

Thankful for a taste of him, she craned her neck upward when he sealed their mouths in a kiss that echoed the joining of their bodies. Holding him inside her for the first time, she felt moisture gather at the corner of her eyes. It had nothing to do with the gentle drizzle supplied by the room.

He stretched her deliciously and complemented her perfectly.

He didn't stop there though. No, simple wasn't Henry Emerson's style.

As he rocked into her with more finesse than power, he

plucked another flexible pipe from the frame. She said, "There's nothing left to tie, Hen."

"Nope." His wicked smile should have been a clue. Still embedded in her and not missing a beat, he aimed the tubing at her. This one had a devious surge that he aimed directly at her clit.

"Ohmygod." Her head rocked from side to side as he kept pumping into her, feeding her more and more of his growing cock while he treated her to delicious pressure that felt like some of the tongues that had licked her in the Basement lobby.

Better, if that were possible.

"You like that." His coo didn't require a verbal response when her body answered for her, hugging him tight within her saturated sheath. "Good. You can come whenever you like, Brooklyn. This isn't some kind of orgasm diet, you know."

The straining tendons in his neck made it clear he yearned to join her. But was she greedy for hoping they could stretch out their pleasure longer? Enjoy each other more before their evening ended?

"Don't worry, there's more to come." He grinned at his own joke.

"Promise?" She whimpered as he shuttled between her thighs, fucking her so well she knew no other lover would ever satisfy.

Even if he hadn't nodded solemnly, she wouldn't have been able to resist when he jiggled the hose he held and added a random splash or two to the steady pattern of the water driving her closer and closer to climax.

As though he couldn't stand their slow, steady grind a moment longer, Henry picked up the pace. Though not violent, his thrusts had an undeniable clout. He pushed into her, giving her all he had and trusting her to take it. The quicker rub of his blunt head against her swollen tissues set sparkles of pleasure dancing through her entire nervous system.

When she still resisted, he mock sighed and reached to the frame once more. Another touch of a button triggered a cascade of sprays from beneath them. One spring welled up between her cheeks and tagged her ass. Other fountains had to have massaged Henry's balls.

He was right with her when she shattered, milking his cock as jet after jet of his come poured into her. He collapsed on top of her, still rocking his hips to feed her every last drop of his release and extend her pleasure.

For long minutes, they kissed as he continued to hump her with tiny strokes that allowed them to savor relief without discomfort to their sensitive flesh. In fact, the embers of her desire glowed brighter with each passing moment.

Brooklyn couldn't believe what she felt. "Are you still hard?"

"Yeah." He seemed almost sheepish about his superhuman abilities.

"You did come, right?" Or had she mistaken his apparent rapture? She'd have had to be dumb to get that tsunami of ecstasy wrong.

"Uh huh." He kissed her, flexing his cock inside her. And just like that she didn't give a shit how, she only cared that his stamina made it possible to have him again. "Not so fast though."

Henry clicked a quick-release on the hoses, unsnapping them all at once. He lifted her and carried her toward the dunk tank.

She practically purred.

"I guess I don't have to ask if you're sure about this then?" He chuckled.

"Just hurry." Brooklyn couldn't believe the desperation he seeded in her. Never before had she been this insatiable, though she knew she had a higher sex drive than most women.

"I will, but you should know that as soon as I activate the hoist above the tank, Oscar will be notified. He personally monitors every scene on this equipment from his office. It's the most risky in the club. Especially with you, nothing unsafe will be tolerated." He winced as if afraid she'd turn back now. "Are you okay with that?"

In response, she lay prone and allowed him to truss her. His expert handling never faltered once as he knotted lengths of purple nylon rope around her. Soon she was hogtied. The clip of carabineers being attached to her rigging sent shivers down her spine.

"So brave." He cupped her chin in his hand as a pulley somewhere elevated her. When she hung over the dunk tank, he paused to admire her. She spun lazily on the end of the rope, unable to resist smiling back when she caught his pleased expression.

The free-floating sensation made her tummy do flip-flops as she swung gently back and forth. That was nothing compared to the exhilaration that rushed through her veins when he lowered her. Water climbed up her legs, over her steaming pussy, and finally to her breasts.

Henry paused her descent there, with her face well out of the water.

But he surprised her when he instructed, "Hold your breath."

A moment later, she had no choice as he grabbed her folded knee and tipped her forward. He let her thrash for a moment before letting go, her own body weight levering her up and out of danger.

Adrenaline flooded her system, fight or flight energy with nowhere to go except straight to her throbbing clit. He treated her to a few more baths, each one slightly longer than the next.

Still, as exhilarating as it was to trust someone this

completely, she knew he was only testing her. Tired of teasing, or maybe having realized she passed with flying colors, he vaulted the edge of the dunk tank and joined her inside.

With her arms and legs so artfully hogtied behind her, all Brooklyn could do was dangle in the water, grateful her head stayed above the waves he caused with his entry.

"Shh. I've got you," he whispered in her ear from behind her. Using the ropes binding her as grips, he positioned her exactly where he wished, then shoved his cock inside her to the hilt with one violent thrust. She would have begged him to do it again and again if it didn't mean he'd have to abandon her pussy first.

Henry roared as he conquered her—this time so different from the last but equally as delicious. Raw power swirled around him, turning her on more. He bit her shoulder and pumped into her a few times, the water making his thrusts slower and more deliberate than they otherwise might have been. As he fucked her harder, water sloshed over the lip.

Still, she craved an edgier passion. She wanted to give him everything, especially if she only had tonight to live out these fantasies. Because she knew she'd never do this again. She'd never go so crazy and have ultimate faith in another man.

"Henry!"

At first he must have thought she was merely screaming his name as he pounded her, fucking her so thoroughly she wondered if she was crazy to need more.

Finally, he seemed to realize what she wanted.

"Are you sure, Brooklyn?" He paused. "You want to go under again? While I'm fucking you?"

Just his uttering the taboo aloud made her shudder.

"I'll come if you do. So hard," she promised.

"Bite me if you need to come up sooner." He wrapped his hand around her mouth, blocking her nose from flooding as well then tipped her forward. The angle not only submerged her, but also aligned his pistoning cock with her G-spot.

Before she could home in on the dazzling ecstasy that inundated her at the revelation, he hauled her upward. Sputtering she shook her head, sluicing water from her hair even as she objected. "More. Longer."

"I won't push too far." He refused to budge on safety, though he never once stopped fucking her.

"You're not…" She couldn't convince him any more when he slapped his hand over her mouth again then held her beneath the surface. The dull *kathump* of her own heartbeat sounded loud in this alternate world. The lack of other sensory input allowed her to focus on his shuttling cock and how far he spread her. How deep he explored.

Brooklyn quaked. Still she couldn't quite manage to come before he lifted her again.

"No." She tried to fight him, to submerge into exceptional territory once more.

"Stop." He smacked her ass as he repositioned her. The wet slap startled her into stillness. "I have something for you. Let me get it."

Brooklyn peeked over her shoulder in time to see him reach for a hose. Different from the ones he'd sprayed her into orgasm with on the waterbed, this one was corrugated. Clear. Instead of talking, he jammed it underwater. A steady stream of bubbles rose to the surface.

Air.

"Open up, Brooklyn." The fierceness of his stare thrilled her. She did as told and parted her lips.

Henry fed her the mouthpiece and she clamped down. No sooner had she secured the lifeline between her lips than he dunked her beneath the waves. She held her breath, instinct screaming at her not to draw water into her lungs.

But as his fucking resumed in earnest, she couldn't help

but gasp.

Fresh, welcome air puffed her chest out.

Brooklyn squeezed Henry's hand, which had taken hold of hers. She knew if she let go, he'd haul her out of there faster than she could blink.

The freedom and security he granted her were priceless.

Though she tried desperately to prolong the rapture, she felt herself tightening impossibly around his shaft. The drilling of his cock opened her wider with every pass. When his strokes became jerky, as if he too were fighting the inevitable, she couldn't take it anymore.

She exploded around him.

Just as Brooklyn worried she might accidentally drop the hose and inhale a lungful of water, Henry lifted her. He hugged her to him as she spasmed and cried out his name. Though he certainly had surpassed every lover she'd ever taken before, even Henry had his limits.

He bulged within her, the veins of his shaft growing prominent enough to impress on her sensitive flesh and enhance her ongoing climax. They also promised he'd join her. She looked down, hoping for a glimpse of him fucking her and instead saw the silvery strands of his come as they overflowed her pussy.

A series of grunts and curses followed as he emptied himself inside her, synchronized to the spasms of her channel around him. Knowing he filled her with jets of his come spurred her to a renewed clenching.

Finally, when they'd both exhausted themselves, he slipped from her grip. A cloud of his seed appeared between her thighs, inspiring an aftershock that wracked her. In a daze, she hardly noticed him untying her until she nearly slipped—completely limp—beneath the surface.

This time she would have drowned. Boneless, she never would have been able to save herself. She shouldn't have worried though. Henry gathered her to him and cradled her against the wall of the tank.

When both of them had regained a fraction of their coordination, he had her hang on to the edge while he climbed out then lifted her from the other side. He carried her through the stream to the pond where they floated, completely blissed out.

Henry tugged her onto his lap as he lounged in the shallows and peppered her with soft kisses. Neither of them spoke. Instead they stared into each other's eyes as rain fell around them and washed the perspiration and the scent of sex from their skin.

Sated, relaxed, Brooklyn laid her head on his chest over his heart and closed her eyes, certain he'd keep her safe. She tried to fight the wave of sleepiness that rolled over her but it was no use.

For once, she knew her dreams would never live up to the night they'd shared.

For the epilogue turn to page 182, *Epilogue: Henry's Surprise (5A)*.

Femdom (4D)

"If you want to be in control, then lead the way." Henry thrust his chest out, inviting her to grab hold of the steel ring in the center of his leather harness. The straps enhanced the golden tone of his skin and drew attention to the cut of his muscles.

When she hesitated, tracing the circle with the tip of one finger, he looked down at her with wide, accepting eyes. "Did you think I was bluffing? You can still change your mind if you want."

"No." She had no intention of backing out now. "I guess I just never expected a man like you to surrender so easily."

"Ah, honey, you've only got me going into the room. You'll have to work to truly dominate our rendezvous. Otherwise, I'll top from below." He winked. "Are you going to let me get away with that?"

"Hell fucking no." She cleared her throat, imagining whipping him for his infractions and insolence. "Henry, if you think I can't do this, you're wrong. Will it change how you see me? Will you want me less if I'm aggressive with you in bed?"

"Don't insult me." His eyes narrowed, causing a dozen tiny crinkles that only added to his charm despite his glower. Then he traced the glittering blue opal at her throat. "Or, worse, yourself. It's a gift—submission. No matter which of us is assuming control or relinquishing it. You know yourself, when you submit, you're really the one with all the power. Besides, you have to be stronger to kneel, don't you think?"

Brooklyn swallowed hard. She nodded. "Then get over here before I have to start our session by leaving my handprints on your gorgeous ass."

His nostrils flared as she hooked her fingers through his harness and hauled him toward the room of her choosing. By allowing her to lead him into the femdom playground in front of every single patron in the Basement, he proved exactly how much respect he had for her.

Never would he have allowed another woman the same honor. Certainly, he never had in all the time she'd worked here. The slow clap that curled around them from their peers said a hell of a lot about them both. A reverent whisper ran through the crowd as they passed. She wondered how many people were taking bets on the outcome of this mash up.

Who did they favor?

Could both of them be winners after tonight? If this had to be her last trip through Underground, she couldn't have asked for more.

Brooklyn unlatched the door and ushered Henry through. She kicked it closed behind them, surprised to find that she could feel in control without the crutch of her uniform or any tools, like the implements hanging in neat rows on the wall beside the entry.

Whips, floggers, paddles, shock wands—you name it, the femdom room had it.

A beefy black bondage bed took up nearly half the space, the sturdy frame obviously built to contain thrashing male specimens as strong as Henry, or the Hulk for that matter. She felt like a spider spinning a luscious web that would eventually entangle them both with no escape except by devouring each other.

Bondage furniture littered the other side of the room. Standard spanking benches, a wooden *X* tipped against the wall, a medical exam table, and a few other lesser-known treats. Good thing she'd taken her job seriously—studying erotic history, attending seminars, and learning from other clients at Underground.

Immediately, the queening stool caught her attention.

She could never get enough of Henry's mouth on her, and he'd seemed to enjoy lapping at her juices a hell of a lot.

"There," she commanded. Henry kept his head bowed and his hands crossed behind his back without her having to order him into the basic pose like a newbie or a sub who pushed buttons for the hell of it. He gave himself completely to her wishes, so she had to nudge him in the direction she had in mind. When he saw the low stool—more like a square, padded seat with the center cut away—and the sling positioned at an angle below it, he grinned.

"When Oscar told me about this thing, I thought I should have one made for my house. But then I figured there was no point since I never take women home," Henry confided in her. "Maybe I'll place that order after all."

He glanced at her from the corners of his eyes. Was he asking her permission? Or simply monitoring her response to see if she'd go stalker psycho on him and assume they were a couple because he'd let her top him once.

"If you like." She stayed noncommittal, refusing to fall into his trap.

Instead of long-term drama, she focused on the immediate future and the ecstasy they were about to share.

"Get on the floor. On your back. You know what to do." And he did. He slid into the lower level of the contraption, his head cushioned comfortably on a triangle of leather suspended from the underside of the stool by a thin chain at each corner. The position left his mouth and nose sticking above seat-level.

When he peered at her from the confines of his voluntary prison, he smiled. "Brooklyn, may I have another taste of you? You're delicious."

"Of course. You did such a good job earlier, I think you must have loved it." She reached through the queening stool to finger comb his hair. Despite his supine position, he still seemed utterly confident. Having a man like him service her...

It was addictive.

"I do." He didn't deny it. Though she spotted his fingers twitching beside him, as if he yearned to reach up and grab her, he stayed where she'd decided he belonged. If she had her way, it would be a forever kind of placement.

"If you make me come in less than three minutes, I'll stroke your cock. For every second you beat the clock, I'll give you my attention instead. Deal?" She began to lower herself but allowed him time to answer, though really there was only a single option.

"Deal," he confirmed.

Brooklyn couldn't say where the instinct came from, but in a flash she reached down and had his nipple pinched between her fingers. She twisted a little, watching his cock jump even as he groaned. "'Yes, ma'am' seems more appropriate."

"Yes…ma'am." He sucked in a breath when she released his tender flesh, so she rubbed the area gently until the disc of his nipple hardened.

Satisfied, she took her place on the stool, adjusting her position unnecessarily to coat his face in her arousal. The incidental swipe of his mouth over her pussy had her ready to scream. Instead, she tried for her best regal voice. "Go on. The clock starts…now."

Henry didn't waste a single instant. He employed tricks she'd never experienced. His face pressed into her so deep, he had to turn his head to the side every now and then to suck in a breath. By the time the clock hit a half minute, she knew he'd have his treat.

And a hell of a lot more of it than she'd imagined possible.

Because before sixty-seconds had gone past, she could hardly keep herself from coming. His tongue thrust up inside her as he ate at her like a starving man. His chin nudged her clit repeatedly and the scruff on his cheeks gently abraded her thighs.

Maybe it was the illusion of control that tipped her over.
But she didn't think so. It was all Henry.

Watching his body flex and strain to pleasure her, she'd
never seen or felt anything as seductive. And though she
clung to sanity as long as possible, her thighs quivering on
the seat with her restraint, when he added a twist of his lips
on her clit to every long lap of his tongue, she lost it. They
split the difference exactly.

He'd broken her in a minute and a half.

Henry had been right. The submissive had all the
control.

With her insides still quaking, she rushed to her feet and
held out her hand. He didn't need it to get up, but he accepted
the symbol of her assistance as he stood upright. The glisten
of his lower face, coated in her come, only added to his
attractiveness. He knew better than to wipe it away.

Brooklyn crooked her finger, and he bent lower. When
she could easily reach, she claimed his mouth in a fierce kiss
that could never fully convey her joy at sharing this night
with him. She sure did try, though.

When he moaned, she snaked her hand between them.
She gathered as much of the moisture from his handsome
face as she could then walked her fingers down his chin,
neck, chest, and abdomen until she could wrap them around
his cock.

"You make quite a handful, Henry." She kissed him
again, though not enough to allow the haze creeping over her
to muddle her concentration. In her mind, she counted the
slow, deliberate pumps she gave his cock as they stared into
each other's eyes.

It shocked her when he began to tremble somewhere
around tug eighty-five.

"Don't you dare lose it." She tried her best to sound
threatening though she'd never hurt him. She might be up for
an agonizing game of edging, though, bringing him to the

brink of orgasm then stopping—maybe all night—before allowing him to gush his release all over them both and thank her for the ultimate intensity.

"Won't." His head dropped back, exposing his neck to her teeth as she counted down the final three pumps of her fist.

When she pulled off him, he roared. His chest heaved and he swayed a little before bringing his gaze back to hers eventually.

"Are you too close to coming, Henry?" She stared into his gorgeous eyes, honestly uncaring if he decided to shoot all over her. Watching euphoria swamp him would be nearly as heady as shattering herself. "Should I calm you down some before we proceed?"

"Yes, please, Brooklyn. I'm sorry. I can't help it. Your pussy tastes so good. I keep hoping you'll let me fuck it." He wooed her with flattery.

"More like *I'm* going to fuck *you* with it." She palmed his cock, noting the long pearlescent strand of pre-come that persisted after she squeezed a drop or three from him onto the floor.

"I definitely need your help." He cleared his throat as he shuffled from foot to foot. The jerk of his erection in her hand let her know how difficult it was for him to stay still instead of humping her fingers for a measure of relief. "Whipping would probably be most effective. I'm not the kind of guy that gets off on pain."

"But you're willing to endure it for me?" She arched a brow.

"It'll help me focus. I want to last as long as I can." He grimaced. "If you fuck me now, I'll come before I'm halfway inside you."

Honestly, she didn't think she would enjoy the thought of hurting him, not even to administer sensual pain. Yet somehow, his sacrifice turned her on. And she found she couldn't say no.

Brooklyn yanked his harness, getting him moving toward the modified Berkley horse. It was an A-framed wooden contraption that resembled a large easel, except instead of a place to rest a painting, it had ankle shackles, a hole for Henry's face, and two rectangles cut in the surface. The configuration would allow him to rest on the board with all his best bits still exposed to her manipulations. One access panel was at chest level while the other left his genitals free to the deliberate discomfort or sensual teasing she chose to administer.

He faltered when she kicked his legs wider apart and his ankles slipped into the leather cuffs. Even unfastened, they had some effect on him.

"You're doing great, Henry." She petted his flank until his shoulders unbunched.

"Don't leave them open." His request stopped just short of begging. "I might not be able to stand still."

She didn't intend to beat him, but sometimes anticipation was part of the fun. Especially for a man like Henry, who could have anything he wanted. She bet he didn't ever have this exhilarating wait-and-see feeling. At least she could give him that much. She squatted and clamped him into the cuffs then did the same to his wrists against the board. Finally, she fastened a thick belt around his lower back to keep him from sagging.

"Thank you, ma'am." His gravelly pleasantry had her checking the state of his cock, still rock hard and leaking.

Brooklyn took her time as she selected a soft doeskin flogger. It was the lightest and softest of all the collection here. Then she pivoted and rested against the wall, taking even longer to admire her slave. If she only had tonight, she wanted to fix this moment in her memory forever. Plus, it made him jumpier when she let him wonder what she was up to.

At the last second, she palmed something else from the wall, unsure if she'd use it.

Without granting him the opportunity to warm up, since she planned to go easy on him—at least when it came to flogging—Brooklyn marched to Henry and let the well-balanced tool in her hand fly. She'd aced her classes, and the refreshers, on whipping. Something about tonight was different though. Never before had this been her election on how to spend an evening with a man. It might become a more frequent pick.

Startled, Henry jerked before he realized the supple strands of the flogger caressed more than stinging or impacting with any sort of bruising force. She laid a dozen additional lashes across his shoulders in an alternating pattern that gave him more time to absorb the sensations she imparted.

When he arched into her next several swings, Brooklyn realized she'd converted him, at least to her mixture—heavy on the pleasure and light on the pain. So she took it one step further.

She knelt behind him, toying with his ass for a moment, encouraged when he pushed back instead of cowering, though by now she expected nothing less from him. Despite what he might have thought she was about to do, she tugged on his heavy sac instead, drawing a groan from him.

Brooklyn repeated the gesture a few times, encouraging the skin there to loosen after being tucked so tight to his core. And when she thought she could make it fit, she snapped a leather ring—a parachute it was called—around the top of his sac. The cone-shaped device encircled his scrotum, and the chains dangling from it made the perfect place to clip weights to stretch him even farther.

"If you're not comfortable with this, tell me now." She scooted around to the inside of the *A* made by the Berkley horse and its legs so that she could establish eye contact. The lust she read in his gaze promised he wouldn't be telling her to stop anytime soon.

"Do it."

She slapped his cock, startling him when the cool chains knocked against the sensitive parts of his anatomy. "Ma'am. Please attach weights. It feels good."

"This was supposed to keep you from coming too fast, remember?" She *tsked* as she drew a line down his impressive length to the slick tip, which still surrendered a drop or two of pre-come on a fairly steady basis.

"Can't help it. It's you, Brooklyn. You turn me on. Whatever you're doing." He didn't play games when he stared straight at her and confessed.

So she decided to reward him for his candor. She gave him what he asked for. Clipping the modest lead bars to the chains wouldn't put him in the big leagues compared to the treatment she'd seen some men endure at Underground, but it seemed effective enough for a beginner.

He thrashed and groaned as his motion only enhanced the sensations.

"There you go," she whispered as she trailed her nails over his shoulder and the faint red slashes she'd left there. "You're going to take one more round. Count them for me."

By the time the flogger cut through the still air enough times for him to make it to double digits, she'd decided that even if he could take more, she couldn't. The gorgeous stallion in front of her made her eager to fuck. If she didn't ride him soon, she'd explode.

And she had one more experiment she wanted to try first...

"Very good, Henry." She kissed between his shoulder blades and then the small of his back as she unclipped the parachute and tossed it to the side. Next, she unshackled the man who'd rocked her world, wrapping her arm around his waist when the belt fell away in case he was off balance.

She shouldn't have worried.

"Where do you want me, ma'am?" He wasted no time, for which she was glad.

"The exam table. On your back with your feet in the stirrups." Brooklyn clipped her instructions to keep him from seeing exactly how hot the idea had her. Sure, it would sting his worked-over shoulders and ass. The reminder would enhance their enjoyment.

His grin insisted she'd failed to tame him.

"Or would you like more here…?" She pretended to consider. "Maybe with an oiled leather crop this time? Or a knotted cat o' nine?"

"No. Of course not." Despite his painfully hard cock, which had a vague purple tinge at this point, he bounded to the exam table and rolled into place with the grace of a lion sunning itself. He only hissed a little when the singing nerves in his back met the leather surface.

His contortion, with his legs up and out wide, allowed her full access to his private region, which she couldn't resist taking advantage of. This time she used nylon bands built into the table to wrap across his chest, ribs, abs, and ankles. He couldn't move an inch as she proved by tickling the sole of his foot. Well and truly held, he moaned when he jerked against the bonds yet didn't break free.

For that matter, so did she.

Brooklyn couldn't help herself. She pumped his cock twice then laid it on his stomach, where it reached nearly to his belly button. A pool of pre-come began to form there.

His stare never once left her when she trailed a finger through the glossy fluid and raised it to her lips to sample his taste. "Mmm."

"Fuck." His head dropped to the surface of the table.

"If you insist." Brooklyn rummaged through the drawers in the exam table, knowing what she was likely to find. "Aha!"

129

She held up an inflatable butt plug and a tube of lubrication for his inspection. His chest rose and fell beneath the restraints as she slicked the rubber, but he didn't object. So she approached, slowly, drawing out the inevitable. And when the blunt tip touched his asshole, she wondered aloud, "Have you ever messed around back here, Henry?"

"No." His response came fast and furious.

"Is Oscar monitoring our session? Do you care if he sees this?" She paused, honestly concerned for any lasting effects of their play tonight. That was her job after all. He'd entrusted her with his safety. All kinds of it.

"Of course. And I don't give a shit." He growled. "I mean... Keep going, ma'am. Please."

Brooklyn flat out laughed, as if she could believe his faux demureness. "Hmm. Maybe next time he'll join us. I heard your whole conversation earlier, remember?"

"He's into guys, but I'm not." Henry didn't blink when he laid it on the line for her. "You can touch me wherever you want. I'm not attracted to men, though if I were, Ozzie would be a decent choice. He's a good person."

"I'm sorry. I didn't mean to put you in a bad spot." She petted his inner thigh, prizing his blatant honesty.

"You didn't." He squirmed, drawing her attention back to where she'd rested the plug against his clenching portal. "Now please, get that thing in there. Ma'am."

"Certainly." She obliged him with one steady push that at first seemed to go nowhere fast. But when she didn't relent, his muscles did, admitting the foreign object. Once it breached his initial resistance, it slid in to the dip near the base that locked it in place.

"Oh, fuck." Henry had been reduced to groans and curses.

Brooklyn probably didn't help when she squeezed the bulb in her hand several times, adding air to the embedded toy. She kept on going, watching his face for the slightest hint of pain. Mild discomfort, yeah, maybe he experienced some of that. But his hips ground down as if they could force the plug deeper as she blew it up more.

"How's that?" She asked as she came to his side, bending down to kiss his parted lips.

He practically ravaged her mouth, giving her all the answer she needed.

"Now Henry..." She tapped his cheek until he opened his eyes and met her gaze directly. "I'm going to fuck you."

"Thank God." He grunted and shifted restlessly.

"But I don't want you to come until we're both ready." She trailed a finger across his collarbones, dipping into the ridges made by his frame and the muscles surrounding it. "Can you do that for me?"

"I'll try, ma'am." He winced. "I hope you don't mind if I start reciting the states in alphabetical order or maybe the serial numbers of all the weapons in our security inventory."

"Whatever it takes, big guy." She patted his abs then climbed onto the table with him. The positioning was a little awkward at first, given the lift of his legs, but she got their pelvises aligned with some good old-fashioned grinding that had them both sweating.

Brooklyn reached between them and aligned his cock with her saturated folds. Each of them cried out when they locked together.

"Wait!" He shook his head like a dog emerging from a pond.

"What's wrong?" She massaged his upper body until he could form a coherent sentence.

"Condom. Put one on me." It wasn't a command so much as a plea.

"I'm in charge here, and I'll decide what's prudent for us both. You know I'm safe. You've seen my file." She stared straight into his eyes. "Tell me, Henry. Is the same true for you?"

"Yes, Brooklyn." He groaned when she reached behind her and grabbed his balls fully in the palm of her hand and squeezed just a bit. "Ma'am. Yes, ma'am."

"Very nice." She leaned forward to buss his lips. She lifted up only enough to aim his cock at her dripping pussy then slowly lowered herself onto him once more. "In that case, in you go."

His heels drummed on the metal brackets capturing them.

Brooklyn understood completely. She had to try several times to fit all of him inside her despite her soaked channel. He was impossibly hard and huge.

When she finally seated herself on him completely, her pussy resting on his torso, they stared at each other. She said what she imagined he was thinking. "Yeah, it's going to be quick."

He nodded, his eyes shut tight.

So she pulled her last trick. Reaching behind her, she flicked a switch on the base of the plug. Soft vibrations echoed in the still room around them. At least until he went wild, moaning and writhing to the extent his bonds permitted.

The ride only got better as he bumped into her and the resulting shockwaves from the plug traveled through his body. She swore she could sense them in the base of his cock as she posted over him again and again. If it would be over soon, she wanted to wrench every last drop of rapture from the experience.

Her pussy clenched on him as she toed the razor's edge of pleasure.

While she wrestled her own passionate response, she never once allowed Henry to be less than foremost in her mind. She monitored the pounding of his pulse, the sweat rolling down his forehead and pectorals, and the flush of his olive skin. Too much more and she'd feel uncomfortable about his safety.

She had to let him off the hook.

"Henry."

When he didn't answer right away, his jaw clenched hard enough to make her worry about his dental work, she slapped his cheek lightly. With his full attention she asked, "Would you like to come in me, Henry?"

"Yes, ma'am." This time he did beg. And it only made her adore him more. "Please. Let me shoot inside you. Fill you up. Fuck. Brooklyn, I need to…"

His desperation for the same thing she required did her in. She bucked over him one last time then ground down hard, fusing them as tight as possible.

Brooklyn came apart in an epic orgasm that Henry couldn't possibly resist. Her pussy milked his thickness, undulating along the entire length of him, drawing his come from his balls and relishing the searing heat of his seed as he doused her pussy with blasts of his release.

Collapsing on top of him, she knitted their lips and kissed him hard. Their stares didn't wander, so she saw the same relief and delight she experienced reflected in his chocolate irises.

Nothing could have given her more satisfaction than that.

"Thank you," she whispered when speech became possible once more. "You were amazing."

"No, you were." He smiled at her, maybe a little sheepish for the first time ever. "Would you mind taking the plug out now? It's kind of…big."

They laughed together as she set him to rights then freed him from the table. He stretched, allowing her to massage his muscles and care for him. The intimate exchange might have been her favorite part of the evening. Until he gathered her in his arms and tumbled them on to the bed.

"You weren't planning on going anywhere tonight, were you?" he asked.

"If you're staying, so am I." She nuzzled his chest and placed tender kisses on the faint mark the strap had made there.

"Good." He resumed some semblance of control. "Then sleep. We can fool around again in the morning."

For the epilogue turn to page 182, *Epilogue: Henry's Surprise (5A)*.

Arc Top (4E)

"It seems like a night for dizzying new heights." Brooklyn glanced up at the stars and thanked them for granting so many of her wishes.

Henry extended his hand to her, palm up. "You're right. It does."

She laid her fingers in his, returning his squeeze as he smiled into her eyes with enough fire and brilliance to rival the heavenly bodies above.

Ever the gentleman in public, he insisted on threading his arm around her waist and hailing a cab for them, though she would gladly have strolled through the streets—oddly tranquil for such an enormous metropolis. No more than thirty seconds later they were tucked into the backseat, her riding in the center because putting any more distance between them than absolutely necessary seemed unbearable.

Fluent French trilled off Henry's tongue. Guttural yet smooth in all the right places, his speech only increased the sophistication he oozed as he lounged, relaxed, in his khakis and light linen shirt. She shifted beside him in a futile attempt to hide how much he turned her on. It didn't matter that she didn't understand a single syllable he uttered despite her language lessons last summer.

Then again, when he turned to her and spoke in English, she still struggled to decipher his meaning through the haze of arousal fogging her better sense. "Brooklyn? Are you all right?"

"I will be." She snuggled into the heat and strength of his chest when he draped his arm across her shoulders. "If our driver would hurry."

"Se dépêcher, s'il vous plaît," Henry requested.

The car lurched forward, squishing her against him. Wouldn't catch her complaining.

To distract herself from the scent of his cologne, which

made her want to lick every exposed inch of his neck, she focused on the scenery flying past outside the cab. They zipped across the river. The fleet of *bateaux* beneath the bridge reminded her of the ride they'd taken earlier.

Had it only been this morning?

Then she got a quick tour of elegant buildings as they soared through a roundabout. Her best guess was that they were heading north, away from the center of the city. She supposed she could have asked Henry, but something about the evening seemed magical, surprises included. So she settled herself and enjoyed the way he twirled her hair around his index finger, staring at her instead of the iconic landscape rolling past the windows.

In less than ten minutes, they entered another traffic circle. This one was enormous, with roads connecting to it like the radii to the center of a crazy spider web. She swiveled her head to glance out the other window, knowing what she'd see. Except instead of the Arc de Triomphe, all she spotted was the square foot of one side. They hadn't made it to this monument today so she'd hoped for a glimpse, but it towered much higher than she'd ever expected. A decent view from the car would be impossible.

Her disappointment only lasted an instant because as soon as he was able, the taxi rolled to a stop by the curb.

Henry paid the driver, including what seemed like a hefty bonus for his speed—worthy of Le Mans. Certainly the man kept repeating, "*Merci,*" as they exited the vehicle.

Brooklyn didn't notice the man pull away. All her attention focused on the colossal arch across the street from where they stood. "Would you mind if we ran over there to take a quick look?"

"Where do you think we're going?" Henry winked at her. "But I don't recommend trying to play Frogger in that mess. There are access tunnels that run below the road. The entrance is right over here."

He led her toward something that could have been a Metro stop.

Signs on the wall listed the times available for visiting the arc's observation deck. They'd ended nearly two hours before. Damn.

When she pointed that out to Henry, he only hummed and nodded solemnly.

While she amused herself with the reliefs carved in the base of the statue, Henry excused himself. She assumed the wine they'd sipped with dinner had gotten to him. However, by the time she'd investigated the horses and battle scenes on two faces of the monument, her date returned with a burly man in a navy uniform that screamed security guard or maybe police.

"Ready?" Henry lifted his elbow away from his body, inviting her to thread her hand through the gap he created, which she did.

She nibbled her lip, regretting they didn't have more time.

"You can check it out in the morning, when the light is better." Henry grinned. Instead of heading away from the arc, he turned them to face it. They followed their escort to a gated door. When the accordioned brass folded to the side, it revealed an incredible spiral staircase that wound up into oblivion.

"It's not as bad as it looks." Henry reassured her. "Under three hundred steps. I've seen you do more in Underground's gym and hardly break a sweat."

The club had facilities for staff to keep in shape and healthy. Another benefit to her job. The one she'd sacrificed...for this.

Might as well make it worth it.

"Race you to the top?" Brooklyn paid no mind to the slight heel on the shoes that had come as part of her temporary wardrobe. She bounded up the stairs on the balls of her feet, with Henry close behind. Their steps echoed in the empty space. It wasn't until they'd circled the tower a half dozen times that she realized the guard hadn't followed.

She peered over her shoulder, then the rail, but couldn't see or hear any trace of the man. With the metal staircase, stealth would have proved impossible.

"He relocked the gate and is watching the front." Henry reassured her as they slowed to catch their breath a bit. "We're alone, Brooklyn. Have the place to ourselves."

"How did you manage that?" Her eyebrows lifted.

"I covered the cost of restoring the rooftop terrace when the historical society fell short on their funding drive last year." He acted like sponsoring such an effort was no grander than tossing a buck in the Salvation Army pot at the mall during Christmas time. "Let's just say they were grateful. We worked out a reward. Come on."

This time it was Henry that seemed overeager as he practically carried her up the next few flights of stairs. Right when the tingling in her calves turned to something uncomfortable, they reached the top.

"Close your eyes," Henry instructed as he came behind her and placed his hands over her face.

She did as told, though normally she didn't appreciate being so out of control. Walking forward, the cool night air swirled around her. Her fingers clutched Henry's as if afraid he might abandon her or let her tip over the edge. The distant din of traffic whirling around far below them emphasized the long drop.

"I'm right here. I've got you. Over this way, a little farther," he murmured in her ear, steering her where he chose. "Okay, now… Look."

It took her eyes a second to adjust to the glitter splashed across the ground like someone had dropped a sack full of diamonds. Henry's arms came around her waist. He hugged her so that his front warmed her back. Before them, a fringing barrier that looked like an enormous comb flipped upside down, ensured they didn't topple over the edge. Not much more held them on the stone terrace that gave her the rush an eagle must get when it perches in its aerie.

"It's...beautiful," she gasped.

"Yes." He tucked a lock of hair behind her ear to keep it from fluttering in the breeze. "You are."

Brooklyn looked at the illuminated Eiffel Tower and imagined the toe-curling kiss he'd laid on her while they'd stared over here from the top observation deck. Looking back at that place, all she could remember was that exhilaration. And she needed to experience it again.

She turned her back on the City of Lights for a man who shone brighter than the millions of stars below them or the smattering of celestial bodies above them. Reaching up on her tiptoes, she wrapped her arms around his neck and drew him to her. It didn't take much to convince him to kiss her.

Their lips met and brushed in a tender series of sips that made her thighs quiver.

"Cold?" Henry broke apart only long enough to ask and rub her arms a bit. Then they were locked together again for a while.

Eventually she whispered, "No," while they caught their breath.

"It'd be a shame not to use the shelter they erected for us." Henry's wicked smile spread until the corners of his mouth perked up.

Brooklyn followed his stare to a cube she hadn't noticed at first. Mirrored on all sides, it blended with the night. "You mean, that's..."

"Mmm." He nodded. "Not usually there. A temporary room. Here, on top of the world. Will you let me make love to you with all the possibilities laid out around us?"

Her heart melted.

Her panties remained in serious danger of soaking as

well.

"Hell, you could fuck me right here for the entire universe to see. I wouldn't mind, Henry." She didn't give a shit about who witnessed the lengths she was willing to go to for this man.

"We'll save voyeurism for Underground, okay?" He kissed the tip of her nose as he guided them toward the refuge.

When he waved her through the door, she couldn't stifle her gasp. It shouldn't have surprised her that no extravagance had been spared. Marie Antoinette herself would have been right at home in the opulent bedding that occupied the majority of the space. Candelabras, made of a metal that shone like solid gold, cast flickering shadows on the one-way glass that made it appear they were still on the rooftop in plain view.

"This is going to be hard to outdo—ever." While she meant in her life in general, he made her heart skip a few more beats when he implied they might have a future.

"I'll do my best to thrill you every day, Brooklyn." He brushed hair off the nape of her neck then kissed her there with a tenderness she wouldn't have associated with the man who stalked Underground some nights.

Maybe both of them had a double-sided nature.

Could they be a perfect fit?

For tonight, she intended to let herself believe so.

Brooklyn kicked off her shoes then shimmied her dress up her thighs, over her torso, and above her breasts as leisurely as she could manage before tossing it in a corner. She climbed several steps to the platform holding the bed above the level of the railing outside their sanctuary. She sank onto the covers and spread herself, wearing only the underwear Henry had arranged for her to model. During the entire show—especially the part where her lace-covered ass was at his eye level—he stared as if prepared to give a standing ovation when she finished.

A growl left his throat as he unbuckled his belt. He let the leather drop to the floor along with his pants, shoes, and socks. Next he threatened the seams of his shirt, ripping it over his head in his haste to join her, nearly naked.

Brooklyn patted the mattress beside her. He skipped the steps and simply laid his palms on the platform then levered himself up with some form of modified push up. His knee hooked over the edge and he joined her in their nest. The smooth motion highlighted the bunched muscles of his arms and the flex of his abdomen.

So much for playing the seductress. Henry had her panting in seconds.

Especially when he reclined on his side, spooning her in front of him so as not to obscure the view. The Eiffel Tower drew her stare like a beacon, reminding her over and over again of the electricity they'd generated between them earlier in the evening. Hell, that one kiss probably had generated enough power to light up the place for the next seventeen years.

As though she might need reminding, he cradled her face in one large hand and turned it toward him. His smile distracted her until his mouth settled on hers. While he kissed her, he rocked his solid cock against her ass, the scraps of their underwear the only thing separating her from what she wanted most.

Brooklyn whimpered, squirming in an attempt to wriggle free of her panties. The skimming of Henry's hand took her bra strap off her shoulder. Then he unhooked the lingerie with a single deft motion that impressed her. He continued his trail, almost tickling the dip of her waist.

When he reached the thin ribbons holding her underwear on, he showed no mercy. A violent yank tore them from her.

A quick lift of his hips and a couple of grunts later, he'd divested himself of his briefs. She wished she could see his

141

cock. Taste it. Please him the way he'd done to her on the jet last night. And this morning. She supposed there would be time for that later.

For now, he allowed the thick length of his shaft to rest between her legs from behind while his mouth traveled from her lips down her neck. By tipping her slightly to her back and plumping her breast closest to his mouth upward, he extended his treatment to her chest. She wasn't about to complain when he took her hardened nipple between his teeth and nibbled. In fact, she arched, feeding him more of the taut flesh.

All the while, she kept her stare on the city landscape that had mesmerized her. Would any of the ant-sized people roaming below have any idea of what they shared so far above the ground?

Henry put one arm beneath her head, creating a pillow of flexed muscle to rest her neck on. She adored being surrounded by him. His chest pressed to her back and his free hand roamed the entirety of her torso, from her breasts to her belly in between forays across her mound and around her clit.

Shivering, she reached for him, grabbing his ass and digging in her nails enough to let him know she was serious.

"Eager?" He nipped her bottom lip, which had protruded in a—she hoped—sexy pout.

"I think I've been very patient," she whispered.

"We both have." Henry traced her smile with the tip of his index finger before sliding it in her mouth. She suckled greedily, thankful for anything to take her mind off the throbbing in her empty pussy. "The time is right tonight, Brooklyn. Just let me put on a condom…"

"No." She stopped him with her vehement denial. "I'm clean. My file at the club and all your fancy testing guarantees it. Plus, you require all the hosts to be on birth control. Why wear protection, Henry? You're safe, right?"

"Do you trust me that much?" He blinked down at her.

"To take my word for it?"

"If I didn't, I wouldn't be about to let you fuck me regardless." She craned her neck to buss his smile. "Please, I want to feel you inside me bare."

"I can't say no." He promised her, "I've never done this before."

"Me either." It felt good to give him something unique. Something special.

"You're sure?" He nuzzled the side of her face.

"Mmm," was all she could manage when he reached through her legs to aim his cock at her opening, using her saliva to lubricate the blunt cap of his dick. If she could have formed a coherent thought, she would have promised him no such measures were necessary.

She'd been wet since they'd left Underground's garden.

Both of them strained toward the other and were rewarded by the tip of his hard-on embedding in her pussy. Relief and a brief discomfort while he spread her wide enough to accept him, simultaneously flared within her and kept her calm enough to take it.

The nip he gave her neck, claiming her in so many ways at once, might have helped, too.

"Ah," he groaned as he fused them more completely with a series of jabs that pressed his hips closer to her ass and increased his penetration bit by bit.

"Finally," she moaned. "Yes."

When he'd gone as far as he could in their position, he slid his hand beneath her knee and lifted her leg, spreading her wide. Both of them rested on their sides. With the city laid out in front of them, a zing of taboo pleasure raced through Brooklyn's veins, carrying the desire Henry inspired with it straight to her heart.

The additional space allowed him to pump deeper within her. She rested against his chest, which rose and fell more rapidly than usual. Free to touch herself, she kneaded her breasts, squeezing and plumping them for Henry's visual delight and her sensory one.

"Christ, you're beautiful." He stared into her eyes with his forehead resting on the side of her face before swooping in for another kiss, this one much more sensual and lingering than the last. All the while he continued to fill her.

Brooklyn couldn't believe the bubbles of rapture he sent fizzling up her spine. Usually it took her considerable manual effort to get herself off, even with the most skilled of lovers. Something about him worked wonders, causing her to lament how quickly this first time would be over.

Please let there be more after tonight.

She didn't ask permission—that wasn't the woman he'd approached—though she felt more submissive with him than she'd ever been in her life before. In control of her sexuality at Underground, she never stopped calculating the next move to make with a guest. Henry erased the need to think. Only acting mattered.

So she followed her instincts.

Brooklyn let her hand slide down her belly to her mound. She cupped herself then split her fingers in a *V* so Henry stroked his cock between them as he rode her from behind. He hissed in her ear when she scissored her hand around him, increasing the pressure he pushed through on every stroke.

After a while, he moved faster, and she couldn't help herself.

Brooklyn shifted her hand. She rubbed maddening circles around her clit with the pads of her fingers.

"That's so sexy, Brook." Henry seemed to surge within her, his cock growing longer and firmer than she thought possible. "I love watching you like this. You're so sure of yourself, so honest about your passion. I could fuck you like this forever."

"Please, do." She meant it, too.

Except no way could she hold on to the live wire arcing between them for much longer.

Perspiration dampened their skin. Their movements grew more and more frantic. And the control they both prized seemed to slip away with each burying of his cock.

"I'm waiting for you, Brooklyn." He kissed her hard, his tongue dueling with hers until they had to break apart or suffocate. "I won't come until you do."

"Really?" She raised a brow, wanting to torture him but knowing it was only a matter of moments before she surrendered to the ecstasy they created together.

"I can feel you trembling, sweetheart." He sighed and drove into her harder, deeper, causing her finger to bounce in the maddening pattern it drew on her own saturated folds. "Let's fly. Together."

How could she resist?

With Paris before her and Henry behind, driving her into the night sky, she let go.

Brooklyn sped the fluttering of her fingers and concentrated on the rasp of the bulging veins on his cock as they illuminated nerve endings inside her. When he dipped his head and kissed her neck, sucking hard enough to mark her—staking his claim—she felt herself begin to fall apart.

She tensed. And then shattered.

The constant drilling of Henry's cock guaranteed they maximized the pleasure of their simultaneous release. When she screamed his name, he echoed with hers. Then the hot rush of his seed flowed into her, washing her in his desire, overflowing her with his release.

For a moment, she thought the lights of the city twinkled brighter, until she realized she'd clamped her eyelids closed to keep from exploding while rapture wracked her over and over.

When she could relax enough to open her eyes once more, it was Henry's face that greeted her.

The awe and reverence in his stare sent aftershocks through her pussy. They radiated through her whole body, converging dangerously near her chest and the heart pounding wildly at its center.

"Brooklyn." He didn't say more than that, but the respect with which he uttered her name knocked her socks off. Or would have if she'd been wearing them. Or anything, really. Lying naked in his arms, she had no desire to get dressed ever again. She could stay here, blissful, until the end of the world for all she cared.

Certainly until morning.

Briefly, she wondered what the tourists would think of the unusual structure on top of the Arc de Triomphe when they arrived to watch the sunrise. And then she realized she didn't care.

Brooklyn drifted off to sleep with a sated smile on her lips. Even better, the last thing she saw as she faded into dreamland was the matching curve of Henry's mouth.

For the epilogue turn to page 187, *Epilogue: Oh Henry! (5B)*

Labyrinth (4F)

"What is it with you and subterranean lairs? You're not a comic book villain, are you?" Brooklyn ran her fingers over the ornate designs in the wrought iron gate covering the ancient oak door. Its pointed arch wasn't very tall, forcing them both to duck as they entered. "Though to be honest, I always liked the dark and dangerous type."

"Unitards aren't really my thing." Though Henry joked, he paused as he withdrew an LED torch from his jacket pocket. The furrows of his brow were enhanced by the contrasting shadows cast by the sun, which rode low on the horizon. With one hand on the door, not yet sealing them in the labyrinth below Paris, he paused. "I guess I never thought about it before. It seems secure. Private. Is it too creepy? We can still go somewhere else. I own three hotels in the city. You could have the best room in the place. Any of them."

"Thank you, but no." She smiled and curled her fingers around his forearm. "I'm curious now. Show me your hideout."

He laughed though they both knew that's what it really was.

Despite their low tone, their voices carried along the rough stone tunnel. Instead of spooking her, the rustic pathway calmed her. Thinking of herself as the next installment in a centuries-long parade of humans somehow made all her doubts and fears seem insignificant.

"I guess I enjoy it here because I feel connected." Henry echoed her thoughts even as his sexy rumble resonated in the passage. "Part of history. Something bigger than myself. More meaningful than a bank full of cash I didn't earn."

Brooklyn knew how wealth could shape your life, distort the importance of things.

When you had everything, it became difficult to appreciate anything.

Except affection. That couldn't be bought or faked well for long.

Henry swung their light so she could peer into a cavern too large to be illuminated by the far reaches of the orb surrounding them. In the distance, she spotted skulls that formed a cross taller than her, surrounded by an entire wall of bones. So many lives. What had been important to these people?

Had they died happy? Did they have someone to love who cared for them in return?

Brooklyn hoped so. She bowed her head for a moment before glancing up at Henry.

Would they make love here, in front of so many witnesses to the joys of life?

"Should I have brought a blanket?" Brooklyn considered the watercolor silk sundress he'd bought for her. She didn't intend to ruin her new favorite outfit, even if that meant strolling through miles of catacombs buck naked.

"Brooklyn, you know me better than that." He touched the back of his knuckles to her cheek. "I enjoy tradition with a modern twist. I'm a man too used to comforts to give them all up now."

Secretly, his admission delighted her.

"Show me." She put her hand in his, and they continued taking turns and twists. Finding her way out without him would be impossible. Around a bend, a larger passageway amplified the trickling of water. A raised stone walkway allowed a stream to run beneath them while a series of gentle waterfalls to the left captivated her. Across a quaint arched bridge, the path ended at a door built into the rock wall. A greenish patina covered the majority of the elaborate detailing in the metal; however, a gleaming *H* shone even in the dim interior of the tunnel.

When Henry's torchlight bounced off the polished surface, she had to squint against the rays flooding her dilated pupils, so she didn't quite see what he did to unlock the portal. Next thing she knew, he ushered her into the private space. The door clanged behind her as he relocked the monstrosity. No one could disturb them.

"Wait here." He kissed her, though it hardly qualified as more than a peck, before crossing the midnight interior of the chamber. With a *whoosh*, a fireplace burst to life, causing shadows to dance on the vaulted ceiling.

True to his word, the plush interior of Henry's hideaway became immediately apparent. Ornate rugs covered what might have been an otherwise chilly floor of shiny Italian marble. Tapestries and paintings as impressive as the ones they'd appreciated in the museums that afternoon decorated the stone walls. A reading nook, complete with a tufted leather chaise and two bookcases, occupied a spot near the fire.

Wandering closer, she inspected his selections. Everything from Poe to Stephen King had a place on his shelves. She imagined this would be the ultimate quiet retreat for a man as in demand as Henry. Shutting out the world would be easy—necessary, too, to regain sanity in his hectic double life.

Brooklyn allowed herself to revel in their isolation, deliberately turning to admire the enormous bed, which served as a centerpiece in the chamber. Maroon silk sheets covered a four-poster bed of some exotic hardwood. The grain of the material practically glowed like a cat's eyes in the amber flare of the fire. Pillows piled high offset the rock surrounding them and called to her with their inviting softness.

She kicked off her shoes and stripped her dress overhead before Henry had returned to her side after lighting a dozen or so candles scattered on tiny platforms that jutted from the walls at various heights. When finished, it seemed as if an army of fireflies bore witness to their liaison.

Henry pivoted. He spied her laid out on his bed like a sacrifice. The breath he sucked in was so sharp, he practically hissed. The pure, honest reaction did more to boost her self-confidence than two years of toying with guests at Underground had. To move a man like Henry Emerson seemed an impossible task.

Yet he came to her side in a flash, tugging at his shirt and the zipper of his slacks simultaneously in his haste to join her.

"Let me." Brooklyn climbed to her knees and began to undo the fine material one button at a time. She kissed the golden skin she revealed with each pass of her fingers. Would he mind her aggression in bed? So far it didn't seem like it.

Although he let her have her way, she still felt as if he had all the control.

Kneeling on the edge of his bed, she admitted she liked that.

When she reached the gap at the top of his unfastened pants, she couldn't help but fish beneath the waistband of his boxer briefs until she cupped his half-hard cock. The initial contact of her hand was enough to plump him more. Still, she couldn't wait to repay his attention from their jet ride last night.

"Get rid of your clothes," Brooklyn demanded.

He didn't argue, though he gingerly stepped away to make sure he didn't injure himself. Her grip regretfully loosened so he could take care of business.

Within a few seconds, he was back. Except this time, he leapt onto the bed and palmed her cheek. "Don't drool, Brooklyn."

She swatted his powerful thigh, wishing she could reach his ass to slap it instead. Maybe one day she'd take him in Underground's femdom room. Shaking her head to clear thoughts of a place she might never step foot in again, she concentrated on her goal. She couldn't deny that she hoped to taste him. Soon.

Brooklyn licked her lips.

Henry smiled and shuffled closer. He held on to the beam connecting two of the bedposts from which a silk canopy draped. "Wouldn't want to get distracted, fall and break my neck before I had a chance to really enjoy what you're offering, sweetheart."

She shook her head as she laughed. "At least it'd be a great way to go."

"True." He wrapped his free hand around his firming cock and gave it a few lazy tugs.

Then all thoughts of witty debate left her mind, replaced by wonder at the heat and zest of his erection as it passed between her lips. He blanked out anything not related to pleasure too, if his groan was any indication.

"Slow, sweetheart." He twined his fingers in her hair, refusing to allow her to take him to the root at once as she would have liked. "Get comfortable first."

Her jaw thanked him as she realized just how thick he could get, even more full than he'd been a moment ago, before she'd tried to swallow him whole.

Retreating a bit, Brooklyn licked at his tip, savoring the slick pre-come that had gathered in the dip there before learning the contours of his frenulum and the web of veins that would feel divine prodding her from the inside.

"Not too much of that." He sighed. "I won't last if you keep…"

He trailed off, intelligent speech replaced by a happy gurgle when she demonstrated some of her skill at giving head. She loved to drive a man wild, and none would make her feel more sexy or powerful than Henry unleashed.

Making him lose his iron willpower would be a rush she'd never forget.

He allowed her to toy with him for some time, not long

enough to suit her though.

When he hovered on the verge of capitulating to the demands of her tongue and lips and gentle suction, she reached between his legs and added the sweep of her fingers across his wrinkled sac, which had drawn tight to his frame.

A spurt of creamy fluid rewarded her efforts.

And then he pounced.

In one swift motion, Henry had sunk to her level, flipped her around and tossed her to the top of the bed. He covered her completely an instant later, the steel of his shaft riding the furrow of her ass. She could so easily imagine him inside her that every fiber of her being yearned to be filled.

"Do you trust me?" he asked.

"Huh?" Her hormone addled wits didn't comprehend what he was asking at first.

"I want to shackle you to my bed. With these." He rattled the chain leading from the stone wall to a pair of cuffs she hadn't even noticed earlier.

Bondage was usually not her thing. Except it seemed that with Henry, everything was her thing. It was him that turned her on and anything they did together seemed a natural extension of that bond.

Brooklyn nodded.

"Say it." He flexed against her bottom, letting her feel the power in his cock. Or maybe he simply couldn't help himself, as moved by their exchange as she was and desperate for relief.

"I want you to tie me up." She whimpered as she realized it was true. Giving him all of her, however he saw fit to use her, would make every second of this encounter unforgettable. Not that it hadn't been already.

Henry kissed the side of her face and made sure she was looking straight into his deep, serious gaze when he said, "Thank you."

Then he snatched the manacle lying nearest her left arm

and got to work.

"I've been wanting to try these out for nearly a decade." He growled in her ear as he buckled the leather restraint around her wrist.

Lined with fur, the cool material held her inescapably, yet comfortably. She wrapped her fingers around the chain linking her to Henry's bed and decided she didn't give a damn about ever breaking free.

"So why didn't you? No other woman brave enough to come down here with you?" She glanced over her shoulder at him as he fastened her other hand.

Serious, he finished binding her, checking the fit and safety of the hold before facing her, still with that solemn look flattening the laugh lines around his eyes and mouth. She wished they'd come back. "I hadn't found the right woman to share this with. This place is special to me, Brooklyn. And so are you."

Unwilling to ruin the night of debauchery with thoughts of reality and what would happen when they got home, she focused on the present.

"Don't make me wait anymore. Please, Henry." It'd been a hell of a long time since she begged for sex. Hell, never. But if he didn't fuck her soon, she wouldn't survive. Waiting was the worst torture.

Brooklyn laid her head on the pillow beneath her, dropped her shoulders, lifted her ass, and spread her knees wide. Whether because of her imploring or the submissive pose, Henry didn't resist. He bounded between her legs and fell to his knees as if worshipping at the altar of her ass.

Henry filled his hands with the taut globes of her backside, squeezing and separating her cheeks as he whispered, "You have a perfect ass. Someday, I'm going to fuck it. You like anal, don't you, Brooklyn?"

"Sometimes." No sense in lying. It'd be obvious from the rooms she'd visited at Underground when the mood struck. "But I haven't done it before with a guy as big as you."

"Good girl." He surprised her with a smack on the right side of her ass that warmed her whole body. The stinging vanished quickly, replaced by the caresses of his palm. "More?"

"Yes, please." She didn't hesitate.

Each spank he delivered dampened the flesh between her legs a little more until she felt a trickle of moisture run down her thigh. Henry must have seen it, too. He groaned then swiped the arousal from her skin.

In her peripheral vision, she spotted him sucking on the thumb he'd used to collect her juices. The bliss causing his eyes to flutter half-closed delighted her. Then he covered her body, blanketing her spine with his heat and delicious weight.

His arms belted around her middle like a harness on a rollercoaster. She didn't mind the suffocation one bit. Then his hands slid up and down. One of them cupped her breast, squeezing with deliberate pulls that made her bow into his hold. His other hand wandered lower until his fingers toyed with her clit. He massaged the dampness there into her flesh as he drew infuriating spirals around the spot where she needed his contact most.

When she thought she might scream from frustration, he added a nip on the crook of her neck to his devious manipulations. Her back arched and Henry lunged. As if they were made to fit together, his cock aligned with her opening.

They both froze when the blunt head of his dick stuck in her pussy the barest bit. Even that was enough to enflame Brooklyn. She cried out then pressed backward, introducing more of his cock to her sensitized channel.

"Jesus. You feel so good. Tight as my fist and twice as hot." He growled as he suckled the spot below her ear with strong enough pulls that she guaranteed he'd leave a pretty purple mark.

No way would she tell him to stop.

Proud of his claim on her, she tilted her head to expose herself more fully.

"Yes," he shouted as he retreated then advanced within her body. It said something to her that it was only then he realized they'd forgotten to use protection. "Brooklyn…I need to get a condom."

"No, you don't." She practically snarled at the thought of him putting something between them. "You know I'm clean from the club's regular exams. Mandatory birth control, too. Remember?"

As if he could forget his own rules.

"Yeah, but I don't have my papers with me." He sucked in a few breaths as if trying to clear his mind. "To show *you*."

"I trust you." Lying would have been futile. "Now fuck me."

"You're sure?"

Brooklyn tried to reach up and bury her fingers in his hair, drawing short when she reached the end of the chain attached to her manacles. The reminder of her bondage thrilled her, causing her to rock backward, taking Henry until he was seated deeper than ever before.

Still she didn't have all of him.

"Okay, sweetheart." He chuckled as the animalist Henry returned, supplying another couple of swats to her ass. "I'll give it to you."

The next few passes of his shuttling hips worked him to the far reaches of her pussy. Finally, he sat completely within her, his body pressed tight to her ass. Joined with her fully for the first time, Henry seemed to relax. His chest expanded against her shoulders when he drew in a deep breath.

"Perfect," he breathed into her ear. "You're everything I've dreamed of and more, Brooklyn."

She might have made a similar declaration if he hadn't

leaned forward, pressing himself as far as possible within her to capture her mouth. Bottomed out, he stretched her.

Henry kissed her as if his life depended on it. Bold swipes of his lips and tongue had her parting to admit him inside her there, too.

Crammed full and held tight in his arms, she allowed herself to float away from all her responsibilities as well as the sadness that sometimes plagued her at being abandoned in this world, alone.

"Yes," he murmured, breaking long enough to catch his breath and reassure her with his lips against her hair. "Like that. Let go, Brooklyn. I've got you. I won't let anything happen to you. Nothing can intrude on us here. It's just you and me and this crazy chemistry we have."

A promise that potent had her pussy wringing his cock. She squeezed him as a ball of ecstasy plopped into her center, causing a ring of pleasure to ripple through her, expanding as it traveled outward from her heart. As if he couldn't resist the response, he began to move. Slowly at first, he tugged himself out of her an inch or two then reintroduced himself gradually, flexing at the apex of his stroke to massage the far reaches of her pussy.

It stretched around Henry's long, thick cock, slickening when he explored depths she'd swear no man had ever reached before. Maybe all the way into her chest where her heart raced as if she'd snorted cocaine instead of relying on the endorphins they triggered in each other for this ultimate high.

It didn't take long before Henry picked up his pace. He began to ride her, causing her breasts to sway beneath her with each tap of his abdomen against her stinging ass. She wondered if she'd be able to see his handprint there tomorrow. She hoped so.

When his strokes grew more vigorous, the momentum allowed his balls to swing forward and tap her clit on every pass. Combined with the pistoning of his cock, the steady pulsing on her engorged nub would have been impossible to resist even if he hadn't chosen then to move one hand from her hips to pinch her nipple.

The bite of intense sensation combined with the fluid glides of his erection drilling her. It rocketed her into an unexpected orgasm. She jerked upward but the restraints kept her from giving Henry a fat lip with the back of her skull.

He roared in triumph as she disintegrated before his eyes. Without pausing, he continued to fuck her through the strongest climax of her life. She had no idea how he was even able to move given the clamping of her pussy on his shaft.

Somehow he managed. Not only did he keep going, riling himself as he witnessed her coming undone, but he somehow managed to keep the embers of her lust glowing even after the most intense waves of orgasm had passed.

"Did you think you were getting off that easy?" He nibbled on her neck again. Sometime his hands had shifted to cup her shoulders from beneath her, holding her in place while he fucked her. She helped by laying her palms flat against the stone, bracing herself against his increasingly hard thrusts.

"I did." She panted. "Get. Off. Easy."

He laughed, though the sound had more in common with the gravel they'd walked on to get here than the smooth smoke of his usual timbre. "My pleasure."

"Hope so." How could he have kept himself from coming when she'd quaked around him?

"Want me to prove it?" He released her now that she'd regained some strength. His fingers gathered her hair and wrapped the informal ponytail around his wrist. Using the tether to ride her harder, faster, he loosened his control enough to allow her a glimpse at his raw passion and the longing they shared for each other.

"Yes!" Her scream reverberated off the chamber walls.

"I'm going to pump my come into your pussy, Brooklyn." He snarled as he plunged to the hilt, making each stroke count. "I'm going to fill you. Overflow you."

She couldn't wait to have another part of him inside her.

"I've never done that with another woman." His confession came somewhat softer.

The admission was enough to poise her on the verge of another epic climax. "I've never allowed a man to fuck me bare."

"Ah, shit. Yes." Henry went into a frenzy. He fucked her like neither of them would get to do this again—not together or at all. While that frightened her a little, the doubt was erased by the possession in his grip and the intensity of his lovemaking.

Just when she thought she couldn't take one more bit of stimulation, she caught him sucking on his thumb in her peripheral vision. Before she could question the odd gesture, with her brain half shut down due to pleasure overload, the thick digit invaded her ass with gentle pressure. Circular rubs that turned into screwing had her scuffing her manicure on the stone wall.

"Good?" he asked as if one word were all he could manage.

"Yes!" She didn't care that she screamed it. "Don't stop."

Then he pressed deeper, working her open until the rings of muscle guarding her entrance surrendered and let him in. He sank a few inches inside her then cursed at the strength of her resulting spasms.

"I can feel my cock fucking your pussy." He groaned.

Brooklyn had never been more turned on. Possessed, controlled and bound, she'd never felt more free. Because she had everything she wanted and all that she needed.

"Come with me." He sounded as if he were gritting his

teeth.

"I'm there. *Here.*" She pushed backward. "With you."

Henry slid the hand not messing with her ass between her legs and flicked her clit with practiced swipes of his middle finger. As if he needed the insurance. If she could have uttered a single coherent phrase, she would have reassured him he didn't.

Brooklyn flew apart, clawing the pillowcase and anything else she could reach given her limited range of motion.

He abandoned her clit to grip her waist tight with the hand not intent on driving her ass insane with rapture. So hard, his clutch probably left bruises she'd wear with pride. And when he grunted, the first gush of warm seed flooding her pussy, he fell forward and bit her shoulder.

Brooklyn prayed it was the claim it felt like.

Together they spasmed and moaned. They cried out each other's names and surfed the shockwaves they generated together for a long time afterward.

It was only the click of him releasing her arms that roused Brooklyn from the daze she'd been in. Glad though, she smiled when he rolled onto his back and gathered her to his chest, which still rose and fell more rapidly than normal.

He tugged a comforter from the foot of the bed over their steaming bodies, which wouldn't take much to chill once the adrenaline of their final dash to ecstasy wore off. Then he kissed her forehead and hugged her tight, encouraging her to snuggle into his strong embrace.

Together they drifted off with matching smiles on their faces.

For the epilogue turn to page 187, *Epilogue: Oh Henry! (5B)*

Sex on the Beach (4G)

"I should make you wait, like you've done to me." Brooklyn sighed, wishing she had more willpower. At least when it came to this man and the effect he had on her. She felt like the needle on a compass, drawn inevitably toward his magnetic north. "But I can't stand another delay. You'll have to show me your cabana later. Take me. Here. Hurry."

"Good choice." Henry smiled wide enough that the whiteness of his teeth rivaled the brilliance of the sun glinting off the smooth surface of the ocean. His expression dazzled her. A hint of uneasiness joined the simmering arousal that pinged between them. After all, he did seem a little like the big bad wolf with that grin.

The better to eat you with, my dear...

All she could do was stare as he approached, slow and sure of his allure. Then the rich walnut of his irises obscured even her peripheral view of the puffy clouds in the distance, the palm fronds dancing in the breeze, and the light material dangling from the corners of their canvas-topped shelter.

Henry consumed her vision and every other sense, too.

The cilantro lime dressing their shrimp had been tossed in tasted even more zesty and delicious when she sampled it from his lips. His knuckles fired nerve endings from her shoulder to her fingertips when he dragged them back and forth as slowly as if they were still beneath the surface of the ocean, impeded by the pressure of saltwater. The hums he made between kisses as his lips roamed down the column of her neck had her pussy clenching.

Soon his teeth took over, first raking her skin then grabbing hold of the ties that secured the tiny triangles of material over her breasts. With a shake of his head, like a sleek shark after its prey, he divested her of the sexy top.

For a moment, he knelt between her legs, plumping the proportional mounds of her chest. Tall and statuesque, she had some decent curves, which he seemed to appreciate. His thumbs skimmed over the hardening tips of her breasts a moment before he licked his lips.

Watching him savor the details of her form boosted her confidence and gave her permission to admire him equally in return. The carved muscles of his pecs and abs could have sold a million gym memberships if he'd been a spokesman.

"You have gorgeous tits," he murmured as he buried his face in her cleavage. His scruff abraded the soft skin there. And she liked it.

Henry soothed the prickle with wet, open-mouthed kisses and the heat of his breath, which came in faster puffs after he tasted her.

Brooklyn took the opportunity to draw on his upper back with her nails. If she marked him, so be it. Laying claim to the man devouring her felt right. He teased her mercilessly, approaching her nipples in a slow spiral that started at the outer curve of her breast. When she couldn't stand his sweet torture another moment, she buried her fingers in his close-cropped hair and tugged.

Aligning him with their mutual goal had the desired effect.

Henry lipped her diamond-hard nipple then suckled until her toes curled—where they dangled off the blanket—into the warm sugary sand. In time to the rhythm he set with his drawing mouth, her hips rocked, wedging her ass into a dip she made in the ground. On the upswing, she pressed her mound tight to his abdomen, rubbing herself shamelessly on his hardness.

"You need more, Brook?" Henry asked after surrendering her nipple with a wet noise that only added to her rocketing passion.

"You know I do." She glared at his self-satisfied smirk. "And so do you."

This time she didn't hesitate. With the assurance she'd

honed at Underground, she reached for the bulge in his tight swim briefs. No hiding there. Especially not a hard-on that impressive.

Brooklyn grabbed his cock through the fabric and squeezed, rippling her fingers so she manipulated him from root to tip. His head dropped back, exposing the thick column of his neck and the flexed tendons there. A shiver went through him as she slipped her hand beneath the waistband to surround him with her bare hand.

"Fine. You're right." He backed away enough to strip the suit from his powerful thighs and elegant calves. A kick launched the trunks behind them, probably into the ocean where they'd be carried away to who knew where.

Good riddance.

Though it'd only been a few hours, she could already see the evidence of the sun working wonders on his bronze skin. The newly exposed patches were several shades lighter than the rest of his amazing body. "I think you should stay like that the remainder of the trip. No need for pesky tan lines."

Brooklyn rose up on her elbows for a better vantage point.

"I'm game if you are." Henry smiled.

Before she could accept his implicit dare, he'd lunged forward and tugged the ties at her hips free. With a powerful overhand throw, her brand new bathing suit joined his on the current, headed for the Ivory Coast.

"Damn. I liked that bikini." She pretended to mope.

"I'll buy you another. For some other time. When we're around people." He dropped beside her and gathered her in his arms, kissing her gently before allowing her to feel the length of him pressed along her frame, not to mention the heavier weight of his engorged cock on her hip. "With me, you stay naked. Deal?"

There would be another rendezvous?

She hoped so.

"Deal." She smiled up at him, feeling secure in another person's hold for the first time since her parents had passed away. Admitting that, even to herself, doubled the stakes of their exchange.

Henry's hand wandered to her newly exposed flesh. He palmed her mound, rubbing light circles on the damp tissue at the apex of her thighs. "You feel so soft. Wet."

"So why don't you fuck me?" A huff escaped before she could regulate her frustration.

"I already am," Henry murmured into her hair. "This is all part of the game. We've been playing it for hours. Hell, years. Don't tell me you haven't noticed me watching you at the club."

Those smoldering stares had been enough foreplay to last a lifetime.

Brooklyn spread her legs. He slipped his hand tighter against her, beginning a maddening cycle of tracing her slit with his middle finger. Every time she chased his skilled digit, he retreated. When she held perfectly still, he rewarded her submission by introducing the tip of the thick finger into her pussy.

"You're tight. So fucking hot." He moaned as he explored. Advancing farther, he embedded his entire finger, then began to swirl it in large circles that had her biting her lip to keep from crying out.

When he added a second finger, she couldn't help but relinquish a needy sound, one she would have hated to make with anyone else. With Henry, it seemed honest.

"Soon I'm going to fill you," he promised.

"Now."

"When you're ready," he insisted, presenting her with a third finger. It burned a little as he scissored them, stretching her channel despite the powerful spasms he was already inducing in her rings of muscle.

"I am," she protested.

"I'll decide that." The stern tone he used on her left no room for argument. Somehow it only turned her on more. She trusted him, she realized. To guide her where it would be most pleasurable for them both.

Brooklyn closed her eyes, relying on him to lead the way.

So it came as a shock when the next thing to touch her swollen folds was his heated breath followed immediately by his tongue. Never would she forget the feel of that clever muscle on her clit.

Henry treated her to a reminder of his talents anyway. He kissed her pussy while his fingers never missed a beat, now gliding from the entrance of her body, where they'd ringed her opening, to the deepest parts of her he could reach.

She'd swear no one had touched her where he did. No one had destroyed her like he could.

He breathed deep, scenting her arousal and holding it in his lungs like the smokers she'd watched at the hookah bar she'd visited in the city once. When she glanced up, the look on his face captivated her. He seemed...peaceful.

Never before had she realized how tightly strung he was. The weight of the club, his charities, and his oath to keep Linley Lane safe weighed heavily on him. More than ever, she was glad she could give him this reprieve.

Not that having a gorgeous man eat her out was any major sacrifice.

As if sensing her thoughts, Henry reapplied himself.

He lapped at her clit then drew the tight bud into his mouth, suckling while he delighted her pussy with fingers that were no match for the tool hanging between his legs. Just the thought of that thick shaft sliding into her for the first time was enough to twitch every muscle in her body, including those hugging his fingers.

Henry looked up at her. The dark fringe of his almost girly lashes lifted high as he surveyed her wanton expression.

164

"Yeah. Come for me, Brooklyn. Come on my face."

His coaching cut off as he buried his mouth in her folds and assaulted her with a barrage of tricks and treats she'd never received the like of before.

Brooklyn's back arched, and she couldn't resist a moment longer.

She screamed his name into the salty air, scaring a marsh bird from the shore with the shockwave of her pleasure. Jerking, her body thrashed on the blanket, kicking sand onto it as she unraveled. Complete abandon assured she didn't feel a thing other than the pulsing of her pussy, which had become the center of her universe.

Still, she reached for the man making it possible.

"Now!" She couldn't stand for him to be separate from her for another instant. If he'd been inside her when she came so hard, she could have died happy. Something was missing.

Him.

"Hang on." He rested his hand on top of hers where she gripped his shoulder like a crab with an unsuspecting fish that had swum too close by.

"No." No more. She refused to defer their joining an instant more.

"I'm not trying to stall you. Just… It'll be better if you're on top." Henry ran a hand through the sand beside them and the mess she'd made of their blanket with her thrashing.

If he fucked her, digging them deeper into the valley she'd created, he would eventually equip himself with essentially a sandpaper cock. Ouch. She figured he had it right, as usual. Her wince must have made him realize they shared the same brain wave.

"Exactly." He tugged her to his chest then rolled until he held her weight fully with his body. Warm and strong beneath her, Henry made the best lounger she'd ever stretched out on.

Melted, she allowed herself to ooze all over him, completely limp. While she regained her wits, she sipped from Henry's lips, taking huge gasps of fresh air between kisses. And when the world returned to sharper focus, with Henry at its center, she smiled.

"I'm a little afraid of that look." He raised a brow, laughing softly.

"You should be." She shoved him when he craned his neck for another lip lock.

His head hit the sand with a dull thud, though he only winced a little as she pounced.

Brooklyn kept him at a distance with straight locked arms that elevated her torso. She let her boobs distract him as she wormed her way south. "Turnabout and all that..."

Although he seemed like he might object, Henry shut his fine mouth the instant she licked a line beside the smattering of dark hair that formed a pretty solid trail below his belly button. By the time she wrapped her hand around him, barely able to make a ring of her fingers given his girth, he'd fisted his hands and clenched his teeth.

"Trying not to come already?" She painted her lips with the tip of his cock, and the moisture beaded there.

"Been holding back since we left the garden at Underground." He groaned when she slipped just the head of his erection into her mouth. "Fuck."

"Soon," she singsonged.

"Hell, for that matter, I've come a lot of nights yanking on myself and imagining you exactly like this." The intensity in his gaze when he forced his head up and eyes open once more blew her away.

No more games.

Brooklyn welcomed him into her mouth with one long, slow, thorough suck. She didn't stop until he was buried so deep he opened her throat. Relaxed—at least she'd found a little relief—she toyed with him, employing all the useful knowledge she'd gained at Underground about how to please a man.

He let her have her fun, bobbing over his entire length long enough to savor the spurt of his pre-come on her tongue a few times. How he held himself back, she had no idea.

But she was glad.

And when he reached for her, hooking his hands beneath her arms and urging her upward, she didn't resist.

Brooklyn climbed his body and settled her knees in the sand on either side of his trim hips. She planted one palm on his chest, using the leverage to lift herself even while she took hold of his saturated cock and aimed it toward her eager pussy.

"Wait." Henry practically growled.

"What this time?" She rolled her eyes, but didn't stop her downward motion.

"Let me get a condom," he barked.

"I'm safe, Hen. You know I am. My file at Underground proves it. We get tested constantly. And you require all your staff get birth control shots." She canted her head. "Or does it bother you? That I've been with a bunch of guys?"

"Fuck no." Henry reached up and cupped her face. "Never let me hear you say that again. I adore your sensuality. I'm only sorry I didn't act sooner. But we both needed…time. This is right. Today is ours."

Brooklyn nodded, trying to dispel the stinging in her eyes.

"But you don't know anything about me." He looked away. "I'm no saint either."

"I know you wouldn't hurt me." She tipped forward until she could kiss him softly. "You're safe, aren't you?"

"Yeah." He met her gaze then. "I just don't have the papers here to prove it. I didn't expect we'd—"

"I trust you." Brooklyn didn't give him another excuse to stop her. She reached between her legs and arched her

167

spine at the same time. As though made for each other—because she was starting to believe they were—he fit perfectly.

The tip of his cock notched inside her pussy.

They stared at each other, no more talking necessary.

In unison they flexed, Brooklyn lowering while Henry fucked upward. His cock penetrated her, burying several inches on the first thrust. Frozen, connected, they groaned as they looked at each other. Then she glanced down at where they were linked.

"All of me," he commanded.

She didn't need to be told twice. Working hard, she lifted then lowered until she'd introduced the entire length of his shaft to her body. Impossibly full from this angle, she sat still, enjoying holding him within her for the first time. Especially after so many wild dreams of this man, she could hardly believe this was real.

When the awe couldn't overpower the demands of her body, Brooklyn began to ride. She swiveled her hips at the height of each rise, driving them both insane. Henry cursed and rested his hands at her waist, helping her post over him as if she were trotting on the fancy horse she used to show before her life had flipped upside down.

Each time she descended, burying him completely, they both moaned.

The weight of her bouncing breasts only enhanced the sensations bombarding her. Brooklyn ground against Henry's torso at the base of each stroke, rubbing her clit on the dense pad of muscle there.

It wouldn't take much more to send her flying again.

"Turn around." Henry nudged her hip. "There's quite a view behind you. Go reverse cowgirl, Brooklyn."

"Maybe I like looking at you." It wasn't a lie.

"There will be plenty of time for that later." He smiled and kissed her before helping her pivot on his cock, which impaled her completely. Damn him, this felt divine. Her favorite position, it allowed the blunt cap of his dick to prod her G-spot.

Within moments, her thighs quivered around his.

Henry helped her, fucking up while she held still. Gradually, he took over.

Brooklyn permitted herself to drift, soaking in the physical delights he imparted while the scenery made a feast for her stare. But when he began to pick up the pace, everything around her went hazy except what he did to her.

As if he knew, Henry urged her to lie back. He cushioned her on his chest and banded his arms about her. With one hand around her neck, keeping her exactly where he wished, and the other teasing her clit, Henry fucked her from below. It didn't matter that she was on top. He possessed her as thoroughly as if he'd bound her. Maybe they could try that sometime.

Brooklyn allowed him to use her as he pleased because it thrilled them. He touched her exactly as they both needed.

His hand never choked her, though she couldn't deny the forbidden ecstasy his hold infused into their desperate lovemaking. And when his thumb pressed on the side of her jaw, she willingly angled her face toward his.

The seal of his mouth on hers wasn't perfect given their contortions and the forceful plunges of his cock within her slick sheath, which rocked her higher on his chest. Still it was enough. A promise of something greater than this insane chemical reaction they produced when they added him and her together. This was affection. Admiration.

Everything rolled into one.

Brooklyn kissed him with every bit of her soul pouring through their dueling lips. She opened her eyes and stared straight into his. No warning necessary. She was going to come, shatter around him and trust him to catch her.

The answering rapture in Henry's chocolate gaze

promised the same.

In fact, the first hot blast of his come inside her might have triggered her orgasm.

Jet after jet of his release sprayed over her pussy, acting like a salve on the inflamed flesh. She tensed then exploded, joining him in rapture. They shouted each other's names, clung to each other, and never once stumbled in the pattern of their undulating bodies. They kept coming together as he filled her, overflowed her.

And though the warm mess he'd made of her would have allowed him to slip effortlessly from her body if he'd sought a quick escape, Henry stayed put. He cradled her on his chest, his fingers petting the pounding pulse in her carotid artery where a moment before he'd clung desperately.

She peeked at him from the corner of her eye, happy to find him gazing at her with an affectionate smile and an air of satisfaction that made her realize just how tightly wound he'd been all the rest of the time she'd known him.

Hopefully she could keep this man. At least a while longer.

She'd never get tired of that look.

Except her body was sleepy, drugged by endorphins, and replete. She never wanted to move. Henry hugged her to him tightly and nuzzled the side of her face.

"Take a nap with me, Brooklyn?" He kissed her forehead and petted her all over with a million insignificant caresses that amounted to a whole lot of something.

"Need to get your strength back?" Was that husky whisper hers?

"Hell, yeah. You didn't think you were getting off with a single fuck, did you?" He chuckled. "Not even a world-class one like that will be enough."

"Mmm," she hummed.

"Rest for a bit." He stroked her hair then sighed when she snuggled into his chest.

With the waves lapping the beach nearby, she drifted off, a smile painted across her face.

For the epilogue turn to page 187, *Epilogue: Oh Henry! (5B)*

Overwater Cabana (4H)

Henry cleared his throat. "Actually, that's only a little cabana. There are a half dozen of them scattered along the beach. The main house is on the other side of the island. I use these for my guests. Or just to get away. Simplify. I didn't want to overwhelm you."

"Ah. Right." Brooklyn considered the stylish building that perched over the ocean on log stilts. It might have been made from native materials, but everything about its thatched roof and mother-of-pearl pool with an infinity edge leading to the ocean below screamed luxury.

Nothing she'd spotted on the *Top Mansions of the World* special she'd watched recently could beat the setup Henry had here in paradise. And there was no one she'd rather enjoy such opulence with.

"Still up for it?" Henry gave her one last chance to bail.

As if she would take it.

Brooklyn grinned. "If you are."

She peeked at his swim trunks, still slightly damp. The tight navy briefs hid nothing.

"I'd say that's a pretty obvious, yes." He didn't delay any longer. "Come on."

Henry took her hand in his. Leading her from their place by the sea, he tugged her into the full sun. Maybe that's why her insides heated near to boiling. The hot sand scorched her feet, teaching her to dance as she rushed to keep up with his long strides.

Where had she left her sandals?

"Doing okay?" Henry glanced over his tan shoulder. When he caught sight of her wince, he stopped and bent his knees. "Sorry, should have realized you're not used to this. Hop on."

Brooklyn hesitated as she considered her height and less than spritely form. Until she assessed the wide expanse of

172

Henry's shoulders and remembered the ease with which he'd hauled their tanks from the dive shack.

What the hell? She figured if they toppled to the ground, at least it would be soft. Screw it. She didn't need a bed to get what she wanted. But the instant she wrapped her legs around his narrow waist and locked her ankles at his front, she realized this was a much better outcome.

Henry broke into a jog as if she was as weightless as they had been underwater. The shifting of his sleek muscles between her legs previewed the delights he had in store for them both. She pressed against him tighter, not in fear that he'd drop her, but because she needed more contact with him. The light scent of salt and perspiration had her licking a line up the thick column of his neck.

Relief spread through her breasts as the heavy tissue pressed against Henry's back. She hadn't realized she'd whimpered until his strained laugh answered the desperate cry.

"Almost there." He bounded up the stairs to the cabana, though she thought he might have referred to their initial joining instead of their physical location. Either way, she was happy.

Brooklyn hardly had a chance to admire the tasteful interior of the cozy retreat, though the glass floor the bed rested on would have been impossible to miss. For one moment she peered into the shallows below, fascinated by the schools of sergeant majors swirling beneath them in a mix of black, white, and yellow flashes.

"You can check out the view later." Henry growled as he set her on the canopied bed. Netting paired with soft linens— all in white—made the bed look like a cloud. She could have been floating in the perfect sky she could glimpse through the wall that opened to the ocean, or the waves beneath it, if she didn't know better.

"I like what I see right now." She took the time to study

him in detail from the dark shadow of his almost-beard to his bare, sandy feet. Even his toes seemed sexy to her.

"Me too." He settled over her, untying her bikini with his teeth, which left his hands free to peel the cups of her top from her breasts. Before she could beg, he'd fastened his mouth over the hardened tip of one and began to suckle while his fingers pinched the puckered nipple of her other breast in a matching rhythm.

Both of them moaned at the contact.

"So sweet," Henry murmured against her flesh when he switched to laving her. Quick flicks of his tongue had her toes curling in the crocheted comforter.

Brooklyn's hands roamed over every bit of him she could reach, from his back to his tight ass. She didn't care if she seemed desperate. She was.

Pride had long ago flown from her arsenal. After everything she'd sacrificed to be here, with him, making love on this gorgeous island, it shouldn't come as any shock to the skilled man now snaking his way down her torso.

His ripped abs stroked her mound, only adding fuel to the fire already blazing out of control within her. Strong fingers caressed her ribs then down to the dip of her waist. Every place he made contact with her skin seemed electrified.

Henry drew spirals around the bows at her hips before grabbing the string on either side in his mouth and tugging until the sparse panel of her bottoms dropped away, revealing her to his hungry stare. Though she couldn't wait to feel Henry inside her—filling and stretching every muscle that already twitched with anticipation—he didn't let her off the hook so easily.

As if she'd forgotten his skill, he demonstrated the aptitude he had for bringing her pleasure with his mouth. When he circled her clit with his tongue, she figured he'd be able to make her come in less than a minute if he really wanted to. Instead, he toyed with her, bringing her close to the edge of orgasm, over and over.

Writhing, she attempted to align herself to best advantage, but his thrusting tongue would dodge after dipping into her entrance. His self-satisfied chuckle had her gritting her teeth. "Quit torturing me."

"I call it delighting." His defense slurred against her slick tissue.

Unable to banter, she spread her legs wider and lifted her pelvis. He accepted her surrender and rewarded her honest passion with the introduction of two fingers into her pussy. The easy glide of the thick digits told them both all they needed to know about the extent of her need.

So did the tremors that began in the muscles of her thighs as she held perfectly still for his manual manipulations. He plunged within her even as he restarted the gentle suction of his lips on her clit.

Without a chance of prolonging the ecstasy he granted her, she surrendered. Bright colors danced behind her scrunched eyelids.

"Yeah." He paused only long enough to encourage her yielding. "That's it. I can feel you tugging on my fingers. I can't wait to feel that tight pussy on my cock. Come for me first. I want to see you fly apart before I can't think of anything but how we fit together."

Oh, shit. Could he tell how much she appreciated a dirty talker in bed?

It'd be kind of hard to miss seeing as how her channel clenched, hugging him tight within her. She didn't need to be told twice. Embracing the rapture he enhanced with each rub of his internal massage, Brooklyn allowed herself to shatter.

She bucked on the bed, trying to embed his hand completely. A powerful climax had her screaming his name and reaching for him to anchor her through the storm of bliss raining around her.

Henry didn't let her down. He extended her pleasure with a sinful figure eight-motion inside her, matched by the swirl of his tongue and the sweep of his mouth over her sensitive flesh. And when she might have collapsed, exhausted and sated, he refused to let her off the hook so easily.

He ripped his swim trunks down his legs, over powerful thighs and graceful calves, before kicking them into the corner. Hell, for all she knew, they'd sailed out the open wall and into the ocean.

Good riddance.

The weight of his cock on her mound had her mewling and reaching for him despite the epic release he'd granted her moments ago. His smile inspired an aftershock that wrung her empty pussy and had her shivering beneath his heavy frame.

Henry braced himself on straight locked arms, which were planted on either side of her shoulders. He lowered himself until he could taste her goofy grin. In the process of kissing the shit out of her, he allowed her a taste of them. Their flavors mingled as she tasted herself on his skin—a fine combination.

Eyes flickering open, she watched as his pupils dilated while they took the kiss to a deeper—more sensual and less hurried—place. Sex with Henry was about more than getting a job done. She enjoyed the connection they shared as much as the physical sensations coursing through her.

From the beginning, he'd identified with both sides of her, public and private. Light and dark. Now she wanted to show him that she understood him, too. That she could satisfy both his civilized and animal tendencies. As if as enamored by their connection as she was, Henry allowed her to linger on his mouth, playing and teasing even as she permitted him to do the same.

Somewhere along the way, they'd both started to move,

the powerful arousal building until neither of them could stay still. As they made out, they ground their bodies together in a tempo she knew they'd ramp up in sync.

She didn't mean to capture him with her restless undulations, but their bodies seemed as if they were made specifically for each other. So when she arched her spine and lifted to meet his next motion, which dragged his cock through the saturated furrow of her pussy, the tip of his erection nudged her opening.

"Ah, shit." His initial elation was replaced with a grimace and an entirely different sounding, "Ah, shit."

"What's wrong?" She barely pulled her mouth away from his long enough to ask.

"I need to get a condom." He lunged for the nightstand but couldn't quite reach from where they'd worked themselves into the opposite corner of the mattress.

"Don't." Brooklyn lifted her hands to his face. She kept his focus on her when she whispered, "You've seen my files from the club. You know I'm clean and on birth control. The requirements are strict for a reason."

"Not so that I can put you at risk by fucking you bareback." His gritted teeth made her think he found the idea hard to resist. "You've never seen *my* file."

"I trust you." She wasn't entirely naïve though. "Are you clean?"

"Yeah." He kissed her again, this time with something sweeter in the mix. "I've never had sex without a condom before. Are you sure?"

"Yes." She looked away for a second, suddenly shy— something that she'd never experienced with a man before. It just wasn't in her nature. "And me either, for the record."

"This means something to you, too?" Henry didn't give her a chance to answer, though his earnest question speared her soul and took her to a place far more dangerous, one where her heart was at risk. Nothing as simple as a thin film of rubber could keep that organ protected.

Instead of proving it with idle words, Brooklyn spread her legs and welcomed Henry deeper into the crook of her thighs. Cradling his hips, she repeated the motion that had positioned him perfectly moments before.

Again the head of his cock nudged her pussy. Only this time, neither of them stopped.

They flexed in unison, Henry feeding several inches of his shaft into her as she rose up to take even more into her greedy sheath. His hiss matched the absolute perfection stealing her breath at the initial fusion of their bodies, and—she'd swear by the determination and longing in his eyes—emotions, too.

Stuck, they stared at each other. Overwhelmed by lust and something richer, Brooklyn shouted out Henry's name when he retreated a fraction of an inch before advancing again, farther this time. He smiled as he claimed her. She could have sworn she heard the word, "finally," buried in his low moan.

Rock after rock brought them together again. Soon they were meshed completely. Instead of a frantic ride, a slow and torturous approach allowed them to savor each twitch that lit Brooklyn up from the inside. If Henry's groans and the fisting of his hands in the rumpled bedspread were any indication, he felt the same.

They continued to stretch out the pleasure until Brooklyn couldn't stand it another moment. She latched her nails into the knotted flesh of Henry's ass and encouraged him to really ride.

He chuckled. "Careful, tiger."

"I need it. I need *you*." At this point it was senseless to be concerned with disguising her urgency.

"Like this?" He teased her, pulling out until barely the tip of his thick cock remained within her grasp before sliding as deep as he could get. The full stroke of his erection on the engorged tissue of her channel had her eyes rolling back, unfocused.

"Again!"

"Yes, Brooklyn." He nipped her neck, causing another spasm to wring her. "You're going to come around me. On me. I want to see it."

"With you." She could hardly form single words anymore, never mind a coherent sentence.

"In a minute. First, show me. How much do you like my cock inside you?" His thrusts became more regular, uniform and deliciously complete. He stroked from her brim to her depths in a ceaseless circuit that drove her wild.

This time a moan was her only response.

And another and another as he guided her upward toward the bright light that might have been the sun outside their utopian shelter or the white-hot ball of lust that would fuel her orgasm.

"Yes." He praised her even as he fucked her, harder and deeper. "Like that. Hold me tight, Brooklyn. Show me how much you need this."

How could she not?

Brooklyn forfeited all her dignity and embraced the base nature he brought out in her. She gave herself over to the rapture, concentrating on squeezing her pussy around his invading cock, making it every bit as good for him as it was for her. At least she hoped so.

Curses fell from his parted lips as he lifted enough to increase his leverage.

By the time she felt his knees dig into the mattress, gaining purchase to shove inside her harder and faster, she didn't think she could stand another minute. Sad at the approach of the end, she tried to cling to bliss. But it was no use.

Brooklyn wrapped her thighs around Henry. The change of angle positioned them perfectly. The blunt cap of his shaft tagged the most sensitive spot inside her pussy. Repeatedly.

A growl burst from her. She sank her teeth into his shoulder, mewling like a wild animal when she exploded around him. Still he continued fucking, never once missing a beat. It surprised her when instead of fading out, her radiant orgasm continued to roll over her in waves that matched the ones pounding the pilings supporting them.

"Fuck, yes." Henry roared as he applied himself to enhancing her reactions.

He sped the shuttling of his hips, lengthened his strokes until he nearly fell from her grasp on every retreat. He powered through the clenching rings of her muscles until neither one of them stood a chance at escaping the inevitable climax they rushed toward.

Together.

"This time I'm coming with you. Going to fill you up." He panted against her neck, licking and nipping as he hammered inside her. His breath gusted against her flesh, fanning the embers of her desire even as he ignited himself. "Get ready, Brooklyn."

"Yes." She hugged him to her, loving the slide of his sweat-slicked pecs against her chest. "I'm with you."

As if her reassurance somehow triggered his release, Henry reared up so they could stare into each other's eyes. His hands latched on to hers, their fingers entwining as he rode her hard, steady, and fast.

With one deep stroke, he reached where no man had before. The complete merger of their bodies impacted them both. Together they climaxed. Brooklyn came around him even as the first jet of his come rained on her inflamed pussy. He bathed her in his release, staying true to his word and overflowing her with the proof of his need.

Their orgasms seemed to go on for hours, both of them cursing, begging, and jerking as rapture zapped them again and again like they'd become human lightning rods accepting the energy generated by each other.

When at last they tumbled into a ball of uncoordinated limbs, Brooklyn couldn't think through the fog of unrelenting contentment long enough to worry about anything. All she could do was seep in the unconditional affection he lavished on her through gentle praise, kisses, and worn-out sighs.

Brooklyn realized she still held him within her, though he'd long ago softened. They fit perfectly, even at rest. A breeze fluttered her damp hair and cooled their steamy skin. The rush of the chop lapping the beams below lulled her. With an enormous smile on her face, she allowed herself to drift off into a peaceful siesta.

For the epilogue turn to page187, *Epilogue: Oh Henry! (5B)*

Epilogue: Henry's Surprise (5A)

"Brooklyn." Henry brushed kisses over her exposed shoulder, drawing her the rest of the way from sleep.

"Mmm." More would have been impossible to say with all the muscles in her body completely lax.

"Have you enjoyed our night as much as I have?" His dark eyes were so serious as they studied her reaction.

"If you can't tell, maybe you should take some of the classes offered here." She couldn't help but tease him. "I can recommend several instructors."

"Then there's only one thing left to settle." Henry grinned. "Will you come back to Underground as manager of the hosts?"

"I don't sleep my way up the chain." Stiffness entered her spine, wondering if she'd gotten things wrong after all.

"Jesus. That's not why I'm promoting you. Hell, Ozzie's had the paperwork done for weeks." The light spank he landed on her bare ass startled her a little and turned her on a lot. This was not the time to mix business with pleasure. "We were waiting for the staff retreat next month to make it official. That was the reason I had your necklace in my desk."

"You swear? It has nothing to do with this." She wiggled her finger in the space between them.

"I promise." He kissed her, seducing her mouth effortlessly. "Though I have to admit, I like the idea of having you all to myself. Or only bringing in a third when we feel like it, not because it's your job to entertain guests."

"So that means you and I..." She didn't want to say it first.

"Are a couple. Yes. That's nonnegotiable." His wolfish grin spoke of how he'd chase her. It made her want to run, if only to get caught. "So how about it? Will you accept the new title?"

"That depends." Brooklyn tapped her swollen lips with one fingernail. "What kind of raise are you going to give me?"

"How about half the club?" Dead serious, he studied her reaction.

"Henry! I couldn't accept that." She dropped her cunning façade. Spending time in such proximity to him wouldn't be torture anymore now that he knew her and, maybe, cared for her. She'd be free to explore with him.

"Okay, fine. Underground is yours. And someday everything else I own will be too." Silencing her objections with a kiss, Henry claimed her mouth until her toes curled and she forgot why they'd been arguing in the first place.

Dazed, she blinked up at the man who'd captivated her dreams for months, only proving to be better in reality than in her imagination.

"You're the star of the show anyway, Brooklyn." He brushed a stray lock of hair from her cheek. "Always have been."

Still, she couldn't believe he'd hand her the keys to his baby so easily. Unless...

"Yeah." He nodded as a smile spread slow and wide across his gorgeous face. The lines around his eyes and mouth grew as he grinned, showing off the square, stubbled jaw she adored, trumped only by the stare he leveled at her. "I mean for it to be ours."

"It's too soon..."

"No. It isn't. I think I waited too long." He shook his head. "Besides, you've already cleared the two highest hurdles for anyone becoming part of my life."

"And what're those?" Brooklyn raised a brow.

"Linley and you get along great." He beamed. "Plus Ozzie thinks you're fantastic. He's been bugging me to ask you out since he hired you."

"Why didn't you?" Brooklyn bit her lip and studied their

hands, entwined completely at the fingers.

"I guess I didn't like how out of control I felt around you. First, there was the instant attraction to your public persona the day I saw you at the Emerson Fund. And then Underground... Well, from the first moment I saw you tapping into a guest's sexuality and enhancing it, I had this gut reaction. Overpowering desire. I'm not used to needing someone else so much." Henry cleared his throat before continuing. "I think it took seeing Linley find her perfect match in a single evening to realize that love at first sight doesn't only happen in fairy tales."

"Well then I'm even more glad you set her up." Brooklyn hugged Henry.

"The only annoying thing about this is how much Ozzie's going to gloat and beat me to death with his 'I told you so' routine."

"I know one way to shut him up." Years in the club had taught her a thing or two about matchmaking. "Keep him occupied. Chasing his own *tail*...if you get what I mean."

"I like the way you think." Henry tugged her to his chest and wrapped his strong arms around her. "And I think I know exactly the right girl *and* guy to tempt him with."

Brooklyn cuddled into her tough yet affectionate lover. A tear slid across her cheek as it finally sank in. She'd gotten lucky. Had it been fate or free will guiding her along the path to ultimate happiness?

Either way, she loved where she'd ended up.

In Henry's embrace.

"Now that I have you, I'm never letting go." He dropped a soft kiss on her crown.

"Me either." She hugged him back, tighter. "So will you let me be there to support you when you break the news to Linley that she's your half sister?"

Henry went completely stiff beneath her, and not in the good way. "How the hell...?"

"It's your eyes. And hers. The same shape. Your other features are similar too. Not to mention how protective you are of her. Without any sexual interest. I've seen the way you watch women…"

"You. I look at you like I want to eat you. Because I do." He relaxed enough to charm her due to the kneading of her fingers on his solid pecs.

"Thanks, but no. You appreciate women. All of them." She hated the spike of jealousy that stabbed her. The affection in his gaze when she lifted her head went a long way toward appeasing her. That was something she'd never seen before. Except when he looked at his sister-slash-boss. "Linley too, but in a totally different way. If you hadn't been related, the two of you would have been an item a long time ago. I heard you tell Ozzie you never guard her ass, remember? And how you referred to her as family in the garden. I know you. The rest was easy to piece together."

"Probably true." He grimaced. "Do you think she'll accept me? When she knows the truth? I don't want to shatter her illusions. I've always known my father wasn't faithful. She never saw her parents like that…"

"Henry." She bracketed his scruffy cheeks in her palms. "She loves you. Linley will be thrilled to gain family, not lose it. Sure, she'll be pissed at first. Hurt, even. That you held out so long. But she'll come around. And I'll be there with you until then."

"I don't know what I did to deserve you, but I'm not going to complain about being the luckiest bastard in the world." He hugged her tight and kissed her temple. "Now enough about that stuff. We can figure it out later."

This time he was hard for all the right reasons.

Brooklyn squirmed on top of him, aligning them precisely. "Make me forget about everything but you."

"That I can do," he promised.

And he did.

Epilogue: Oh Henry! (5B)

"Brooklyn." Henry brushed kisses over her exposed shoulder, drawing her the rest of the way from sleep.

"Mmm." More would have been impossible to say with all the muscles in her body completely lax.

"Have you enjoyed our weekend away as much as I have?" His dark eyes were so serious as they studied her reaction.

"If you can't tell, maybe you should take some of the classes offered at Underground." She couldn't help but tease him.

"Good." He drew his hand from behind his back, holding a small box he must have grabbed while she dozed.

"What's that?" She shook off the remaining tendrils of laziness begging her to return to sleep and rubbed her eyes for a better look at the velvet cube he opened and turned to face her.

"A congratulations present." His smile widened in proportion to her eyes, which had to have grown twice as large when she spotted the blue opal pendant she'd resisted splurging on while shopping with Linley one afternoon. The platinum teardrop setting enhanced the brilliance of the stone.

"Wait. What?" She sat up a little and tipped her head. "I mean you were great and all but does that warrant a pat on the back?"

He laughed when she thought he might get pissed instead. "Thanks. But, no. It's for when you agree to come back to Underground as manager of the hosts. I don't want there to be any mistakes. Everyone will know you're mine."

"I don't sleep my way up the chain." Stiffness entered her spine, wondering if she'd gotten things wrong after all.

"Jesus. That's not why I'm promoting you. Hell, Ozzie's had the paperwork done for weeks." The light spank he

186

landed on her bare ass startled her a little and turned her on a lot. This was not the time to mix business with pleasure. "We were waiting for the staff retreat next month to make it official."

"You swear? It has nothing to do with this." She wiggled her finger in the space between them.

"I promise." He kissed her, seducing her mouth effortlessly. "Though I have to admit, I like the idea of having you all to myself. Or only bringing in a third when we feel like it, not because it's your job to entertain guests."

"So that means you and I..." She didn't want to say it first.

"Are a couple. Yes. That's nonnegotiable." His wolfish grin spoke of how he'd chase her. It made her want to run, if only to get caught. "So how about it? Will you accept the new title? And my gift?"

"That depends." Brooklyn tapped her swollen lips with one fingernail. "What kind of raise are you going to give me?"

"How about half the club?" Dead serious, he studied her reaction.

"Henry! I couldn't accept that." She dropped her cunning façade. Spending time in such proximity to him wouldn't be torture anymore now that he knew her and, maybe, cared for her. She'd be free to explore with him.

"Okay, fine. Underground is yours. And someday everything else I own will be too." Silencing her objections with a kiss, Henry claimed her mouth until her toes curled and she forgot why they'd been arguing in the first place. Once she'd gone complacent, he slipped the chain around her neck and fastened the clasp. The weight of the stone felt perfect at the base of her throat.

Dazed, she blinked up at the man who'd captivated her dreams for months, only proving to be better in reality than in her imagination.

"You're the star of the show anyway, Brooklyn." He brushed a stray lock of hair from her cheek. "Always have been."

Still, she couldn't believe he'd hand her the keys to his baby so easily. Unless...

"Yeah." He nodded as a smile spread slow and wide across his gorgeous face. The lines around his eyes and mouth grew as he grinned, showing off the square, stubbled jaw she adored, trumped only by the stare he leveled at her. "I mean for it to be ours."

"It's too soon..."

"No. It isn't. I think I waited too long." He shook his head. "Besides, you've already cleared the two highest hurdles for anyone becoming part of my life."

"And what're those?" Brooklyn raised a brow.

"Linley and you get along great." He beamed. "Plus Ozzie thinks you're fantastic. He's been bugging me to ask you out since he hired you."

"Why didn't you?" Brooklyn bit her lip and studied their hands, entwined completely at the fingers.

"I guess I didn't like how out of control I felt around you. First, there was the instant attraction to your public persona the day I saw you at the Emerson Fund. And then Underground... Well, from the first moment I saw you tapping into a guest's sexuality and enhancing it, I had this gut reaction. Overpowering desire. I'm not used to needing someone else so much." Henry cleared his throat before continuing. "I think it took seeing Linley find her perfect match in a single evening to realize that love at first sight doesn't only happen in fairy tales."

"Well then I'm even more glad you set her up." Brooklyn hugged Henry.

"The only annoying thing about this is how much Ozzie's going to gloat and beat me to death with his 'I told you so' routine."

"I know one way to shut him up." Years in the club had taught her a thing or two about matchmaking. "Keep him occupied. Chasing his own *tail*…if you get what I mean."

"I like the way you think." Henry tugged her to his chest and wrapped his strong arms around her. "And I think I know exactly the right girl *and* guy to tempt him with."

Brooklyn cuddled into her tough yet affectionate lover. A tear slid across her cheek as it finally sank in. She'd gotten lucky. Had it been fate or free will guiding her along the path to ultimate happiness?

Either way, she loved where she'd ended up.

In Henry's embrace.

"Now that I have you, I'm never letting go." He dropped a soft kiss on her crown.

"Me either." She hugged him back, tighter. "So will you let me be there to support you when you break the news to Linley that she's your half sister?"

Henry went completely stiff beneath her, and not in the good way. "How the hell…?"

"It's your eyes. And hers. The same shape. Your other features are similar too. Not to mention how protective you are of her. Without any sexual interest. I've seen the way you watch women…"

"You. I look at you like I want to eat you. Because I do." He relaxed enough to tease her due to the kneading of her fingers on his solid pecs.

"Thanks, but no. You appreciate women. All of them." She hated the spike of jealousy that stabbed her. The affection in his gaze when she lifted her head went a long way toward appeasing her. That was something she'd never seen before. Except when he looked at his sister-slash-boss. "Linley too, but in a totally different way. If you hadn't been related, the two of you would have been an item a long time ago. I heard you tell Ozzie you never guard her ass, remember? And how you referred to her as family in the garden. I know you. The rest was easy to piece together."

"Probably true." He grimaced. "Do you think she'll accept me? When she knows the truth? I don't want to shatter her illusions. I've always known my father wasn't faithful. She never saw her parents like that..."

"Henry." She cupped his scruffy cheeks in her palms. "She loves you. Linley will be thrilled to gain family, not lose it. Sure, she'll be pissed at first. Hurt, even. That you held out so long. But she'll come around. And I'll be there with you until then."

"I don't know what I did to deserve you, but I'm not going to complain about being the luckiest bastard in the world." He hugged her tight and kissed her temple. "Now enough about that stuff. We can figure it out later."

This time he was hard for all the right reasons.

Brooklyn squirmed on top of him, aligning them precisely. "Make me forget about everything but you."

"That I can do," he promised.

And he did.

About Jayne Rylon

Jayne Rylon is a New York Times and USA Today bestselling author. She received the 2011 Romantic Times Reviewers' Choice Award for Best Indie Erotic Romance. Her stories used to begin as daydreams in seemingly endless business meetings, but now she is a full time author, who employs the skills she learned during her straight-laced corporate existence in the business of writing. She lives in Ohio with two cats and her husband, who both inspires her fantasies and supports her career. When she can escape her purple office, she loves to travel the world, avoid speeding tickets in her beloved Sky, and, of course, read.

Jayne loves to chat with fans. You can find her at the following places when she's procrastinating:

Twitter: JayneRylon
Facebook: http://www.facebook.com/jayne.rylon
Email: contact@jaynerylon.com

You can also sign up for her newsletter at the link below. One winner of a prize pack is drawn at random from the Naughty News subscribers for each issue sent.

Newsletter sign-up: http://bit.ly/Y523Db

Other Books By Jayne Rylon

Available Now

COMPASS BROTHERS
Northern Exposure
Southern Comfort
Eastern Ambitions
Western Ties

COMPASS GIRLS
Winter's Thaw
Hope Springs

COUGAR CHALLENGE
Driven
Shifting Gears

HOT RODS
King Cobra
Mustang Sally

MEN IN BLUE
Night is Darkest
Razor's Edge
Mistress's Master

PICK YOUR PLEASURES
Pick Your Pleasure
Pick Your Pleasure 2

PLAY DOCTOR
Dream Machine
Healing Touch

POWERTOOLS
Kate's Crew
Morgan's Surprise
Kayla's Gift
Devon's Pair
Nailed To The Wall
Hammer It Home

RED LIGHT (STAR)
Through My Window
Star of Christmas
Can't Buy Love
Free For All

SINGLE TITLES
Nice and Naughty
Picture Perfect
Phoenix Incantation
Where There's Smoke

IN PRINT
A Little Vamp
Cougarlicious
Dream Machine
Eastern Ambitions
Love's Compass
Mistress's Master
Needing A Cougar
Night is Darkest
Pick Your Pleasure
Pick Your Pleasure 2
Powertools
Razor's Edge
Red Light
Three's Company

Two To Tango
Watching It All
Western Ties

AUDIOBOOKS
Powertools – anthology of Powertools Books 1-4
Kate's Crew
Morgan's Surprise
Kayla's Gift
Devon's Pair

Coming Soon

COMPASS GIRLS
Sizzlin' Summer
Falling Softly

HOT RODS
Super Nova
Rebel On The Run
Swinger Style
Barracuda's Heart

MEN IN BLUE
Spread Your Wings

PICK YOUR PLEASURES
Pick Your Pleasure 3

PLAY DOCTOR
Developing Desire

IN PRINT
Healing Touch
Hope Springs

Hot Rods
Love Under Construction
Pick Your Pleasure 3
Winter's Thaw

Made in the USA
Columbia, SC
08 July 2022

63078963R00109